Praise

"The women who inhabit Heather Marshall's *Between Sea and Sky* embody a fierce persistence, moving through their worlds with an unwavering sense of self and a profound connection to the natural world. Marshall crafts each narrative as an intimate portrait of resilience, her prose marked by both imaginative depth and emotional insight. These stories exert an irresistible pull, drawing readers deeply into their world."

Carla Damron, author of *The Weird Girl*

"I stopped reading short stories years ago because they seemed cold and intellectual, and oftentimes nonsensical to me. But these stories are warm and rich, full of emotion and human experience. And the sense of place is strong, so detailed it is obvious the author knows and loves it as her own. The characters conquer fear and life's heartbreaks through that connection to place and to the people they love. The stories are gifts for the soul, and I am grateful for having been given the opportunity to read them."

Maureen Nery, author of *Saving Grace*

About the Author

Heather G. Marshall is a Scottish-American author, speaker, and teacher. She is the author of two novels, *The Thorn Tree* and *When the Ocean Flies*. Her short fiction and essays have been published in a variety of journals, including *Black Middens: New Writing Scotland*, and *Quarried*, an anthology of the best three decades of *Pine Mountain Sand & Gravel*. Her TED talk, "Letting Go of Expectations," centers around her adoption and reunion.

heathergmarshall.com

Between Sea *and* Sky

Heather G. Marshall

Between Sea and Sky

Print Edition
ISBN: 978-3-98832-224-1
Published by Vine Leaves Press 2026

Cover design by Jessica Bell
Interior design by Amie McCracken

For Corey, Dylan and Davis

Contents

Substrata

Remember when we rode down the hill beside the primary school, legs stuck out because the pedals on our fixed-wheel bikes turned too fast for us to keep up? Remember the bite of the rain on our cheeks, red and chapped from being out in that harsh winter? Remember coming in? You do, don't you? We dripped a muddy puddle on the floor, tried to mop it up, the pair of us wiping those hopelessly large sheepskin mittens and woolly scarves across it, trying to make it right and instead smearing mud into the wood and the wool runner.

"Go," you said, there on your knees, "before he gets here."

I couldn't. It was my puddle too. Besides, I had nearly an hour until dinnertime. What would I have said if I'd walked in the back door, found my mother standing at the kitchen counter, paper spread open, as usual, reading other people's horoscopes? That I'd made a mess and then run away, abandoned my friend to his father, the front room, the choosing of a belt.

He came in, curly hair like yours bouncing on top of his head, his white to your blond, and asked what you'd done. The next part, and the next, I'm sure we'd both rather not remember.

Was this the beginning?

What I remember is being left alone in the room with his father, waiting, straining for a sound of my best friend down the hall. The racket of my own heart banged; my blood swooshed in my ears. I got hotter and hotter as I stood under the gaze of Craig's father. It seemed ages before I heard the creak of the hall cupboard door, so faint I might have conjured it for respite. Mr. Sullivan tipped back on his heels, clasped his hands behind him as the slight clink of the belt buckles bumping reached the front room. His face softened. I thought he might smile, plump out his cheeks and show his teeth, yellowed and dull. He rocked a little, heel to toe in his heavy brown lace-ups, striped tie swinging out and back.

I don't write this—I haven't come all this way to drag Craig through my experience of his pain—I skip instead to what happened next.

Afterward, you told me the trick was to pick one broad and thick enough to satisfy him. Too flimsy and he'd go back and get the worst of the lot. You had to gauge him in the moments he marched you to the front room, made you name the infraction. Did you wonder if you might have selected a flimsier belt? Suffered a little less?

The belt dangled from Craig's hand, shaking. His father commanded him to unzip his trousers, pull them down, bend. Craig's face turned the color of the poppies we sold for Remembrance Day. I turned away.

"You are to watch, young lady."

I watched Craig's father. I pulled every ounce of defiance into my eyes, held his. It took me over a decade to realize that was what he wanted. The belt flashed across my vision, cracked against Craig's skin. I held still, rooted, unflinching. My body jumped within itself as he swung once, twice, again, ten times.

"You will pay attention the next time you enter this house." He dropped the belt. He smiled. He left. I heard the ice, two cubes, clink into his glass. I heard the slosh of liquid that followed, then another, fizzy sound.

I went to the window, rain streaking down, while you pulled up your trousers, slid up the zipper, put back the belt. You came to stand beside me, slid your chapped fingers into mine.

"Sorry." We said it at the same time.

Remember?

I had to go. By then, I was late for dinner and wishing I had the kind of mother who would come roaring down the hill, bang on the door and ask had they not the common courtesy to send a child home on time?

We switched to walking in the woods after that. Spring would be coming soon. We'd found those hatchlings the year before. For years, I thought I was the one who decided to look for old nests in the bare trees. Now I wonder, had it started by then? Was it nests you wanted or the safest places to build them?

In my recollection, we decided to set out the next day, on foot, into the woods, a pad and a pen and a tape recorder to take down our observations: the size of the nest, materials, the surrounding trees. First, we knelt, side by side on the skinny bed in your room. I loved the feel of the two of us huddled in that little bump-out in the attic. What is it—ten feet by ten feet? I think we were both glad Michael—the only one of your four siblings still at home—wasn't around that day.

We opened the book of birds, read sparrow, robin, thrush, blushed at each of the tits—blue, coal, crested, great, long-tailed, marsh, willow. We read about ones who migrate, who weather the winter, look for last year's nest and ones who build them freshly every time, abandoning the old.

By the time the buds on the trees began to unravel, we were back on our bikes, thinking ourselves very grown up at twelve years old, needing a wider range to roam. We coasted down Kilmabry Road, heads tilted back to watch a hawk catch invisible drifts of wind. By summer, we wanted the shore, sixteen miles, one way, farther than you were allowed. We both knew the risk.

While I packed sandwiches and then pushed him out the back door, my mother stood with her finger on Virgo, proclaiming something about the moon's transit in Venus and Craig's brilliance shining through. I could see her, through the window, still standing there when we rolled off into the street. How long did it take her to realize we were gone?

On the shore, the waves wandered the sea up around us. Farther out, a lone puffin, bright beaked, spotted us too late and scurried back to his nest between the rocks. You sat on your haunches, clutched knees to chest. "He's too far south," you whispered. You said you feared for the little bird, at our latitude, just below Scotland's waist, N 55°34'33", and him building his nest all alone.

Later, the *he* struck me. It sounded like an assumption my father would make. I stopped at the top of the hill on Mannock Road, panting. "How do you know it was a he?"

Craig smiled as though I was years younger than he. "It's always the male Atlantic Puffin who builds the nest." He pushed off, took four strong pedal strokes and then coasted down the other side of the hill, his heft putting easy distance between us.

Was it that year that you found the house martins nesting in a hole under the eaves near your room? You said they are supposed to nest in cliffs like puffins? Pushed out of their natural habitats, they make do with holes in houses, offices, whatever presents itself. Was it then that you told me that fossils of puffins have been found from thirty-four million years ago? That they have adapted their wings and feathers to be able to swim underwater? Or was it three years later, when we boarded the train to Fife, and then the ferry to the Isle of May to see them, safe with their colony of thousands, in their farthest south habitat, N 56°11'16"? I thought, with the power of public transport, you would soon be safely away from him. Now I see it had already taken root.

You huddled in the belly of the ferry, recited facts about how much difference degrees of latitude might make and what other factors matter.

On the island, you settled us beneath a sheltering crag. We watched the puffins waddle in and out of nests the males had tunneled into the soft strata beside the rocks.

"They live in there, one male and one female, for life," you said. The wind lifted your curls in all directions. "He lines the burrow with grass and leaves for her. And then she lays just the one egg." You took my hand, entwined your long fingers with mine. "They take turns holding the egg against their brood patch with their wings."

I laughed at brood patch, made some comment about a love patch, and tugged at yours, the only facial hair you had then. You laughed, too, explained about the birds losing feathers on their bellies near the end of the egg-laying period, about the supplemental set of vessels that bring the blood supply to the surface of the skin to help keep the offspring warm, about the regrowing of the feathers to keep the adults warm at sea.

"We're lucky to see them here," you said. "Normally, puffins don't find the proper place to thrive below Caithness, at N 58°25'00"."

When did you begin to become stuck at the latitude of your room? What other factors might have made a difference?

We went again, before my father started my westward migration. He moved the three of us to various cities on the East Coast of the United States. No matter where we landed, we sat at three sides of our huge, polished table. It seemed to get larger at each new location. My mother read his horoscope when she served his evening meal. When I was young, he used to tell her which parts were correct. By the time of the migration, he'd taken to staring straight ahead, one hand planted on each side of his plate, pressing hard against the gleaming wood, as my mother read.

The first few years, we came back annually, but not at the same time each year. On our last trip, we didn't even sit together on the plane. My mother found three seats on which to stretch herself. My father, one over from me, shut his eyes before we were airborne. Later, I came alone.

I felt like a bird, migrating back and forth over the open sea, in the wrong seasons and with the bright beak of summer long gone.

Do you remember the next-to-last time? I wrote to you that I had followed a boy to Chicago, become pregnant, then abandoned, that I had booked the airfare. You drew a map to the place where I had the termination.

We spilled out of a multi-level car park in the city center into a tight throng. Craig's pace quickened immediately. I struggled to keep track of his blond curls, bobbing ahead of me as he maneuvered too deftly between people, like someone possessed.

What were you thinking when I grabbed your arm as we released from the crowd, turned down that narrow alley and felt the press of rain-soaked sandstone on either side of us? Was that safer for you?

"Stop," I said, pulling him close. My breath was heavy. A wave of nausea began to rise. "You don't have to be here." I let go, bent and pressed my palms against my thighs. I spoke mostly to Craig's knees, noticing the bony marks in his jeans, faded places that indicated he had been kneeling or else sitting for a long time on his haunches. "I can find my own way home," I said.

You bent, lower than I, looked up into my face. Were you on the brink of tears?

"I want to be here," you said. You stood. "It's so hard." Your clenched fist hung at my eye level.

I thought you were disgusted with me.

On that second trip to Caithness, Craig had told me that his father had explained how some girls became soiled goods. According to him, just the sex act made a girl too stained to claim. What, then, did that make me?

On the way back to your house, suddenly struck by a compulsion to stand in open air, I clutched your knee. "Stop. I have to get out." I ran around to the driver's side and pulled you out. You took three gasping breaths and then bolted to the holly trees at the edge of the woods where we had rested as children.

Standing between the holly and chestnut, you pointed to two nests, one low, near the trunk of the chestnut, the other messy, high, near the edge of a branch. "Look how different they are, Nellie," you said. You shimmied away from me, into the branches of the chestnut. I called out to you, saying you could come, escape, migrate with me. "Did you know that all the chestnuts in America are dead?" you said. Your back was to me, head tilted slightly back.

Craig's father, by then, had begun to shake when he held the belt. The last time I saw him, he was sipping his first gin of the day, neat, looking so true in the cut glass tumbler. He needed both hands to hold on, there at the shiny table, eyebrows furrowed, knocking it back, then thumping the glass down on the table. A little sloshed over the side. He put one finger in the liquid, making the dots join.

"Mother," he yelled. "Mess."

She started out from the kitchen, wiping her hands on her apron, dark eyes shining.

"I'll do it, Mum," Craig said.

"Do it right."

While Craig wiped, his father stood, pushed back the chair, left it out from the table. He caught my eye, smiled his yellow smile, and marched out the back door. I almost exhaled, and then he returned, bending to nestle his head on Craig's mother's shoulder and reaching around her with a bunch of perfect honeysuckle blossoms he must have plucked from the vines that grew, wild, just outside the high, brick wall that enclosed their back garden.

After that time in the chestnut trees, I drove, alone, from Chicago, west. I don't remember what roads I took, with the few belongings that mattered crammed into my hatchback, to get to the edge of the continent. Your photo, propped on my dash, led me. I stopped at N 45°52'54", nearly 10° south of where I began. If my mother read any of this in the horoscopes, she has given no indication.

I came one more time after that, at Christmas time. I stood on the front steps and asked you to go to Caithness.

"If you'd said that's what you wanted," you said. "I could have planned."

You put one hand on each of my elbows, pulled me inside, closed the door and then pushed me into the front room. Beside the hearth stood the same silver tree that had been there when we were children. You took my hand, your fingers still long and smooth as I remembered them, and so perfectly warm.

"Nell," Craig said. He faced me, his curls still thick and a little too long, shrouding his face.

"Craig," his father's voice, following the thump of the glass, hurtled down the hall.

I couldn't watch what it had become.

"Come with me," I said.

"Craig," the voice this time accompanied by the rhythm of footsteps.

I slid into Craig's hand a slip of paper bearing my new address. "Haven't you always wanted to fly?"

When I first left, you wrote page after page, your familiar script tight and tidy, yet ignoring the lines on pages torn from school jotters. I still have all your letters, tied in a bundle.

Craig's mother contacted me, nearly a decade after that last migratory journey. *Dear Nell,* she typed, in an email. *I hope this is the right Nell. Please reply, even if you want to hear no more, or are unwilling to do as I ask.* She'd racked her brain to think of what had got him out of his room in the past. *Didn't you two have an afternoon in Glasgow?* It was the farthest, apparently, Craig had been since the agoraphobic episodes began.

Did your mother tell you I was coming? Did you get my letter? She isn't sure.

She says Craig has been in there for a month since his father died. He took his place in the receiving line at the funeral. As the crowd moved toward them, Craig walked briskly away. They thought he would come out in a day or a week, as he had before. Michael suspects that he climbs out the window and moves from ledge to ledge down the side of the house. No one has actually seen this.

The last season you wrote, a spring, a rainy one for me, some years after my last migration, each of your letters contained only

an image of a nest or an egg or a bird. The last featured a bird tumbling from a nest, one wing outstretched.

I didn't know how to reply.

I'm sorry.

The excuse I gave myself was that my father had tired of my mother reading his future to him. Perhaps she was, too often, wrong. Or right. He remarried and moved to Maine. My mother migrated south. She lives in Florida, at N 27°56', her skin growing hard and dark. I imagine her a turtle, huddled near the dunes, her lone hatchling having scurried toward the sea in the moonlight, floated away, not returning to lay her own eggs. Mother still reads horoscopes. She calls when there's doom or love on the horizon. I left her clucking to my voice mail, closed the door on her predictions to cross the broad body of land and then the wide sea to return to where I began. I realize, now, how well I have adapted to my new latitude. How long will I be able to sit here outside his door, feeding notes underneath, waiting for a sighting?

Will you come with me now? Will you come to Cannon Beach? Sit with me on the edge of another continent? We can carry our memories there, build a fire on the beach in the evening, toss the pages we'd like to shed on the flames, watch the edges blacken and curl. Come with me and watch our ashes rise, watch the wind pull them away. There is always a breeze. In the morning, we can awaken, there on the beach, just before dawn. You can slip your hand in mine as we walk to Haystack Rock, where the tufted

puffins nest. By the time the town rises, they will have returned to their tunnels, safely cradled within the rock itself. We can watch as they scurry in, these tufted puffins, not quite so round as the ones we watched years ago, and with comical yellow tufts on their heads.

When tufted puffins make their nests, when they dig their tunnels into the strata, through the grass and soil and into the soft heart of the rock, the female works just as hard as the male. They are lovely to see.

Within

Glasgow, Scotland. 1966

The Putative Father, as he will become known, waits. When the Mother, as she will be documented, spills out onto the street with the other student nurses after exams, the Putative Father sneaks up behind her, wrapping his hands over her eyes. The Mother then lets the Putative Father steer her back to his room for one last moment before they share themselves and their secret with their families over the Christmas holidays.

"I want to watch you open my prezzie here," he whispers, letting her go for only the moment it takes him to retrieve the parcel from under his bed.

She smiles, glad of the moment, a kind of present itself, so they won't have to do this at one of their homes after the trail of Santa gifts for their younger siblings.

She pushes back her dark, straight hair, letting it cascade down her back, and then she pulls off the ribbon and pulls back the tape and pulls out a robe, which he wraps around her, red and plush, a sort of shag number, velvety and perfect for 1966 and her growing body.

"Just a wee thing," he whispers, turning her around in his arms, there in the dingy dormitory at Glasgow University. Outside the door, the hallway is unusually quiet, most of the students having already scurried out the door toward home and holidays. Outside the window, rain spatters down as afternoon hurtles toward darkness.

The Putative Father tightens his arms, and the robe, around the Mother. She snuggles up, feeling the caress of his wavy hair and mutton chop sideburns. There, wrapped within his strong arms and within the soft robe and within herself and the gift she thinks they are, she feels their baby growing, not yet showing, but so safe and loved inside the robe and him and her, right in the center of them.

She nearly makes them miss the train. Or he nearly makes them miss the train, but blames it on her, saying how could he resist with her wrapping herself right round him and looking so gorgeous in that red robe.

They pack themselves back up quickly afterward, tucking shirts into jeans and presents into suitcases and running, hand in hand, down Sauchiehall Street and into Queen Street Station, panting onto the train and collapsing into their seats, ignoring the people around them.

"That's not good for the baby," she whispers.

"Acht, it'll get him ready for the rugby," he says it out loud, hand on her tummy, already the proud daddy.

His mother's words lasso around them.

"You will not," she says to him, there in the front room of his house on the other coast of Scotland.

Behind his mother, white lace curtains hang in the windows. On the arms and headrest of her chair, and every other sitting surface in the room, white lace doilies brace for the touch of a human arm or head and all the germs and dead skin and loose hairs that come with it.

Outside the door, his siblings scrabble for position at the keyhole. Outside the window, the sun strains, trying to slide through clouds and lace and spotless glass. All the gifts have been given and received, two days ago.

His mother turns to him, straightening her hand-knitted, white lace cardigan, "You. Are the brains of this family. I will not," his mother leers at the Mother, "see him give away his future on Some Baby."

His mother says more, her words spattering down, syllable on syllable until the sun sinks and the lace looms, luminous and triumphant against the darkness.

The Mother wraps the yarn around her fingers and then around the knitting pins—through, around, over, out, again and again. She is making baby clothes by the front window at the Mothering Home. She is making clothes for Jayne. She chose the name after her favorite aunt; added the "y" because some of the other girls at the home said Jane was too ordinary; reminded her that the baby wouldn't know it was her favorite aunt. Jayne, she says it to herself as she knits. She likes the feel of the word, especially with the "y" added. *Exotic.*

Outside the door, other girls sob against the Home Mother's rhythmic, "This is best. This is best. This is best." Outside the window, light and dark dance, the dark losing ground day by day until her daughter comes, two weeks early, a sunny afternoon in April. She wraps the baby in the clothes she knitted.

She gives the baby; she gives Jayne away.

She keeps the robe; wraps its shaggy softness around her loss; tucks it into its box, leaving the loss cradled in the center, the way her daughter once was in the middle of the robe and of her and of him.

As Good as a Feast

In the night, rain. Lilly realizes this when she steps outside for the pints of milk. Plump bubbles glisten on the silver caps. She resists an impulse to bend and suck them off. Instead, she imagines them, cool and soothing as they slide down her throat. Lilly breathes in as deeply as she can, which isn't very deeply at all these days.

Water gushes along the curb; this has been no gentle drizzle. Lilly slept through it, a small miracle, for which she is grateful. If only she'd been aware of her sleep. It must have been delicious, smooth and lovely.

For the past month, she has chased sleep night after night, lying awake while Robert has rolled over and dropped off straight away. Lilly stares at the ceiling in these dark nights, one ear trained on wee Hugh in the next room. He never makes a peep. Instead, her own heartbeat thuds, steady against the baby's erratic kicks inside her. Lilly's other ear strains for the warning of distant engines approaching; her mind imagines the whizz of the buzzbombs. Robert's contented snores offer a background drone to it all. She lies still. Blackout curtains seal them all in tight, seal out any hope of light. Is this what it's like for her baby?

Lilly lifts the milk, wipes first one and then the other bottle, and watches the clear drops fly; her thirst builds. If she tilted the bottle to drink the clear droplets, she would cause the cream to mix in with the rest of the milk. Such a small movement, sometimes all that's needed to alter everything. Lilly imagines the good cream slipping down, dissolving into the milk, irretrievable. She holds a pint in each hand, steady, and turns toward the door.

At the kitchen sink, she pours the cream from the pint bottle to a small cup. The rich, thick consistency is something on which she can rely. This has become Lilly's daily ritual, reserving the cream for Hugh. He's four, a slim boy, never having been a chubby-cheeked baby like those pushed in their prams by so many other mothers. On Hugh, the cream won't go to fat, only keep him from being too lean—keep him strong—in this time of rations.

The cream off and set aside, Lilly pours the milk into her favorite porcelain jug. Her eldest sister gave it to her on her last visit home to Belfast. *How long will it be before she can get back across the waters to them?* Lilly covers the jug with a circle of embroidered white cloth. Another sister sewed beads around the edges to weight the cloth, holding it closely over the milk. This protects it from flies and anything else that might sneak past.

Lilly rests, one hand on top of her belly, the other on top of the thick slab of wood. Both seem larger than they ought. Her belly is swollen with a child that feels as close to coming as the bombs that whistle in her imagination in the dark. The wood is part of a table-cum-bomb shelter. Robert made it so he could slide mattresses under it and shelter them on nights when the sirens sound. Lilly recalls his long, muscular arms with the saw, back muscles visible through his shirt. He believes the table will protect them from any falling debris. From the moment her father handed her to Robert at the altar, Lilly has believed that Robert would be her strength, her shelter. As she watched his strong hands wrap around the heavy wood, she felt the doubt rise.

"Are we not better going to the shelter, as we've been told?"

Robert lifted the solid piece of wood. "This is better than the three of us scurrying down the street in the dark in the hopes of reaching an air raid shelter and then having to huddle inside with god knows who," he said. Beads of sweat clustered around his hairline.

Four, Lilly thought. *The four of us.* She rubbed her tummy, the merest protrusion then—just a hint of the child to come.

Lilly rubs her belly now, feels the child, big enough for a bent limb to be recognizable to the touch, still within her, for the moment. She wants to believe as Robert does. She wants to believe that the bombs will cease before the Luftwaffe takes aim at targets other than London.

As she turns toward the larder, she takes a faint contraction with her. It hasn't the urgency of labor yet—hasn't the strength that requires her to count its length or the space between this one and the next. There will be a long space, days maybe, before another contraction. She tries to distract herself from wondering how long before this, how long before the next bomb, or the space between them, by taking stock.

In August, they still had tomatoes and vegetables from the garden to round the rations up to something substantive. By the end of September, there were enough to count at a glance. The one bomb came then, early in the month. No more since. Still, the memory lingers.

Lilly looks at the larder, counts the potatoes; one, two, three.

The whistle first, then the thud.

The wee bit of flour.

The target missed.

Lilly tots up in her head how much she can make do with for Robert's dinner.

The reports in the paper, from London, of night after fractured night. Rigorous blackouts. The Luftwaffe finding key targets: hospitals, government buildings, railway station after railway station.

She tells herself they are lucky to be in Crewe, the railway station big enough that they want Robert here, but not so attractive a target as London; she tells herself she is lucky to be still separating cream from milk for Hugh. Children in London were evacuated a year ago. She knows, though, that the effects of war don't just wound those who live near bomb sites. She lifts the lid on the porridge, calls to tell Robert his breakfast is ready. She heaps the thick oats into his bowl, to keep him going through the morning's work at the railway station. *At least we are all together.*

Waiting at the table for Robert, she recalls the whole big family of her childhood in Belfast, the clatter of feet coming to the table—Daddy and Granny Hughes and Lilly's brothers and sisters. Mummy standing at one end of the table, waiting as the steam rose from the plates. She was one of the few on the street who didn't work. More than once, she'd reminded Daddy, always at the dinner table, that she could be working in the linen mills to earn the family a few extra pounds.

"Wee Lilly wouldn't have to spend her whole life in cast-off dungarees and dresses," she said.

"I've a skill," Daddy said. "I'll not have people saying Big Oliver Hughes's wife has to work. Have you not clothes on your back? A roof over your head? Food in your belly and a fire to warm you?"

"We could have..."

Last time she said this, Daddy put down his knife and fork, silently, balanced on the edges of his plate.

"Where would that end?" he put his hands flat on the table.

Everyone paused, stilled their knives and forks and silenced their chatter.

"There will always be more *we could have*. We've enough." Daddy lifted just the fork, speared a sausage. Juice oozed out the side. He knifed a mound of buttery potatoes on top of the sausage, held it in front of his mouth. "Enough." He slid in the sausage and tatties, full lips sealing around them. He chewed slowly, took his time swallowing. "And enough's as good as a feast."

Mummy nodded, just the once. She closed her lips, dabbed them, put the napkin back on her knee and smoothed it.

When the sirens sound again, Lilly thinks, at first, it's a false call. Robert wakes from his sleep and responds faster than she. In complete darkness, he takes her hand. They feel their way into Hugh's room. Lilly gathers the boy, hands him to Robert, who leads them down the narrow stairs. Lilly hangs on to the back of Robert's pajama shirt. The three of them huddle under the table, so close that they are like one multi-limbed animal. In the dark, Lilly thinks she can see Hugh's eyes, bright with excitement. There, under the table, safe with his mum and dad, he thinks the bombs are a thrill. He's seen the photos in the paper and heard snatches of news on the transistor. No one he knows has been hurt by one yet. He holds his eyes wide as long as he can, until they snap shut and his head goes heavy on Lilly's belly. Kicks and punches from his impending brother or sister don't stir him. There is the whistle. There is the thud, close. The vibration. Lilly closes her eyes. The blackness is the same, eyes opened or closed. She waits, breath stilled, an arm around Hugh, Robert's long limbs entwined with them. She can hardly tell who's who. The air stills. The table goes untested.

How long they wait is hard to tell. Darkness makes the minutes stretch. Nights are long now. At length, Robert unfurls his limbs, lifts Hugh. They make their way back up the stairs.

After breakfast, after Robert leaves, Lilly barely has her bum on the seat for a rest when Hugh bounds down the stairs.

"Can we go, Mummy? Can we? Please?"

It's all she can do to get a bit of her freshly baked Irish wheaten bread, buttered, down his throat, washed down with the cream. He's back up the stairs and struggling into his clothes—trousers on backward when he comes back down. He nearly vibrates with excitement as she gets him sorted.

Hugh takes his mother's hand and pulls her out. He drags her arm to its full extension as she locks the door. The faint scent of smoke hangs in the air. Women gather on the street corners; they murmur their tales of shelter, squint at the weak sun. Closer to the site, people move slowly, linking arms and pulling close together.

Hugh's eyes bulge when they arrive. He looks at the crater as though he's looking at a dent made by a cosmic beach ball—a freak thing on show at a fun fair—rather than a buzz bomb. He tries to free himself from her hand. Lilly holds tighter. A small contraction starts.

"Please, Mummy, please." Hugh squats, free hand touching the earth at the edge.

Lilly looks down at Hugh; she recalls being Hugh's age and looking down at her brother, John, his hands on the earth. She'd been perched on top of her eldest brother's shoulders. Her first clear memory: herself and Davey and John at the unveiling of the *Titanic*.

Only Davey had really wanted to go, but Mummy insisted he take the lot of them. As they made their way down the garden path, Lilly hadn't cared one way or another about the *Titanic*, only she wished she was holding her mother's hand instead of her brothers', as was often the case. One hand in John's and the other in Davey's, Lilly's left side stretched higher than her right, and a wee bit out in front as they made their way down the lane away from the house—two gangly boys with a plump wee girl in the middle, dark curls bouncing, feet feeling as though they barely touched the ground. The sisters strolled far behind. Had there been an option for seeing the ship's maiden voyage, they might have had an interest. That was months away, though, and it wasn't going to happen in Belfast. The sisters would have been far more interested in who got on the vessel—the ladies with their smooth pearls around their necks, diamonds glinting in the sun, the men in their crisp coats and hats and ties—than they were in the ship herself.

Mummy had said they all had to go and look out for each other. Really, though, they were going so Mummy could have the place to herself, and maybe get in a wee bit of a natter with Mrs. Scullion next door. Mummy always seemed eager to have them out and away.

The crowd was already thick when they arrived. Davey put Lilly on his shoulders. Not for her own sake, but so she could tell what she saw. Even he wasn't tall enough to see over caps and hats and bonnets. Up there, looking out over the sea of people to the vessel that was to take the water, Lilly imagined Mummy still at home, quietly smoothing things, windows open, feet firmly on the ground. How lovely it would be in that stillness instead of waving about like a flag on top of the shoulders of a brother on tiptoe, weaving side to side to see for himself, obviously without much success, or he wouldn't have kept her there, nor kept at her with his questions, as he did.

"What's it like, Lilly?"

"Big."

"Is it shiny?"

"A bit."

"A bit? What d'ye mean, a bit? Has it towers like the papers said?"

"No."

"No? How can it not have towers? Are you sure, Lil? Are there sailors on board? What are they doing? Have they uniforms? Do you not know this is the biggest ship in the world? It's going to sail right the way across the Atlantic."

How could she have missed it with him prattling on day after day?

"D'you know where the name came from Lil? Greek gods. They ruled the world."

"God rules the world, Davey." Lilly patted his head. "And Jesus."

He tilted his head back. "I know that, Lil. But in school, we read the stories of the Greeks."

She looked down, past Davey's eyes. There was John, digging.

"Don't tell Mummy I said it," Davey said.

"Put me down, so."

Lilly recalls the feel of him lifting her off his shoulders, of her feet landing on the solid earth, next to John, her tiny hand on dark ground next to John's already broad one.

Standing in front of the crater, Lilly keeps hold of Hugh's hand; she slowly lowers herself to meet him. She breathes in the dusty air, the sharp scent of dying embers. She dares herself to touch the damaged earth.

When Lilly hears the next air raid siren, she wishes for the warmth of Robert's body beside her. Instead, she has the cold steel of the hospital bed rail to grasp. Lilly thinks of Robert and Hugh under the table; Robert's long arm, ginger hairs prickly, wrapped around Hugh's small body. At the apex of a contraction, she imagines the bomb striking, layers falling in—roof, ceiling, floor, table—all encapsulating them. She has an impulse to dig down, to search for the comfort of dark earth. She recalls John running out and away after school, nicking Davey's bike often, and even Daddy's once, riding out into the countryside, digging and digging. He came home with pockets full of rocks, lay them out on his bed, examining each one carefully before deciding which ones were worthy of his scant space on the bookshelf. After Mummy smacked him sore (because of the dirty mess he made on the freshly cleaned quilt) and he had to eat dinner with his bum half an inch off the seat, legs shaking from the effort of it, he stashed them under the bed. Like a gigantic cat, he drew his long body under and bent himself to fit so he could turn the rocks over and over, making muffled commentary. On days when she'd tired of following Mummy, Lilly crawled under and scrunched with him. She didn't care about the rocks but loved the heat of his whispered breath in the scant light, the warmth of his body as she curled against him.

She puts her hands on her belly, notices her own warmth.

"That's a good girl," the nurse says. "Maybe you'll get a lovely little girl this time." The nurse smiles too big a smile. It makes Lilly's cheeks hurt. Boy or girl doesn't matter to Lilly. She wants the child brought from womb to world, safe and whole. It would be too much to bear if this baby pushed forth from the layers within her on the same night as his father and brother became fossilized in their home.

"Damn this war," Lilly says, not meaning it to be aloud.

"There, there, Mrs. Murray." The nurse's voice is high. "We're safe in here." She pats Lilly's hand.

As though she was five again, Lilly aches for her mother's hand, the rare feel of those long fingers on hands that seemed nearly always to be busy elsewhere. She stretches out her hand, sees it as if it isn't her own. It looks like a smaller version of John's, less hairy, thank goodness. Lilly recalls the feel of her small hand in John's rough one as he guided her fingers across the one fossil he found, in the same year they saw the *Titanic*.

"A real live fossil." His voice was just a whisper.

Lilly scrunched her face, bent to the rock. "A live rock?" Her eyes widened. Lilly hadn't been to school yet, or any other place that might have taught her about something as exotic as fossils. Thus far, her education consisted of always saying please and thank you, gathering the weekly wash and transporting it to the washroom without leaving a trail. She'd recently learned to use the handbeaters to froth the meringues on special Sundays, and she was fully in charge of putting away the low-lying bowls in the kitchen.

"No. Course it's not a-live. It's a rock. See?" He lifted it and held it right under her nose.

She stood as straight as she could. "You said 'a real, live, fossil'."

"Anyone with half a brain would know I meant an actual fossil not an alive one, Lil. You're not going to grow up thick, are you, Lil? Mum not save any brains for you?"

Lilly felt her small throat tighten. She began to crawl out. "I've got work to do. I'm not so thick as to get my bum thrashed over some silly rock."

"Ah wait, Lil," he took her arm, gently. "It's just. Look here, in the rock." He lifted her hand again, rubbed it gently over the surface. "Feel that? That's the bones of an actual animal, lived here thousands of years ago. Imagine! Got itself trapped in the rock, perfectly preserved. At least I think that's what's happened. I'll take it to the master tomorrow. Isn't it marvelous, Lil?"

She smiled up at him. What was marvelous was a boy who could grin from ear to ear over a rock, and who told her first about his prize. Who cared if he called her thick along the way?

"It is." She gave him a wee kiss on the cheek.

A sudden, harsh contraction brings her back to the nurse, the hospital, the steel rail. The nurse lifts her hand, squeezes it, too hard. She smiles her gigantic smile, again. Everything seems at once too tight and stretched too far. There hardly seems to be a gap between the pains. Lilly's mind leaps back and back to angry snatches of memory: her father and Davey across the table, the morning paper neatly folded with the image of the *Lusitania* on it. Davey had been drawn to it, loving boats as he did. His face crumpled as he read of the boat sailing homeward, nearly there.

As the next contraction takes her, Lilly imagines the torpedo shooting through the dark waters. She hadn't understood when she was a girl. Even watching Daddy and Davey's angry faces, she'd felt safe, thought her family distant from the danger in the paper. The contraction releases. Lilly tries to pull herself back to the present, to her breath, to the baby.

She hasn't gathered herself when the next contraction comes. Snatches of argument roll in with it. Daddy telling Davey he couldn't enlist, just weeks after the *Lusitania* sank. Mummy standing, frozen, rashers of bacon crisp on their plates. Potato scones lined up neatly beside them. "It's done," Davey said. "I'm away. You can't expect me to stay here, content with scraps. Britain rules the world, Da. And you can't stop *me* from having part of it." More than the words, Lilly recalls the smell of freshly fried lard, her bit of bacon catching in her throat, Daddy's red face, fists at either side of his plate. Mummy's pinch-faced powerlessness. Davey going first, then John, sneaking out three days later. He'd lied about his age. The pair of them floated away, leaving the family severed.

She does not resist when, at last, the nurse puts the mask over her face. Lilly makes a last feeble grasp for her belly. She drifts.

The child squawks into the world at five pounds, even smaller than his brother was at birth, but plenty big for Lilly's small frame. *His* food, at least, will not be rationed. There will be no need to separate cream from milk for two for a while yet.

In the morning, the metal springs on the bed creak as she presses herself upright, her arms reaching for her son before the nurse is halfway down the ward. Perhaps because he's the last baby handed out from the nursery, or perhaps because Lilly's bed is closest to the window, the nurse stays at her bedside. Lilly holds the baby to her, feeling both of them more fragile in the presence of the nurse, a square woman with tentacles of frizzy hair escaping her cap; her broad body blocks some of the rare light. Lilly wishes she would go. Another nurse joins her by the window. She wants them both to go; she wants the baby all to herself before Robert strides in. Did her mother ever feel that?

"That's 430 more dead in London," the first nurse says.

Lilly tries to focus on her son, to ignore their conversation.

"430. Imagine." She continues, shaking her head. The tentacles shiver. "And that's not the worst of it."

Lilly wants to close her eyes, the way she did when they brought the news of Davey. And then of John. Her mother had. Closed her eyes, pulled her hand from Lilly's, flung both hands up to her face, turned and fled. Lilly had lifted her eyes to the sergeant. She lifts her eyes now, to the nurses. She faces their too-pink lips moving. Is lipstick allowed?

"250,000, homeless."

Lilly imagines the people tiptoeing back to their houses, seeing the shell of what once was, picking through the charred remains, finding what they can and being forced to leave the rest to the wind and the rain and the coming years, whole lives covered over.

"Five railway stations."

"Five," Lilly whispers. She thinks of Robert at his work. Should she worry? And what about Hugh? He'll be with Mrs.

Adams, next door, by now. Has he been a good boy? Will Mrs. Adams hold his hand if they go out? Part of her wants to know more. Part of her wants to shout at the nurses, to tell them to be quiet, to ask why they are saying these awful things.

The baby begins to root. One nurse turns to her.

"Poor thing, born into this," she says.

A foreign feeling rises within Lilly, an indignation tinged with determination. "Not a poor thing," she wants to say. "My son. Whom I'll see grow strong."

She parts her lips to speak. The baby lets out a squawk; the sense subsides.

The nurses' shoes squeak as they walk back down the ward. The baby settles in for a first feed. Lilly holds his gaze, thinking of the rail travelers, getting on and never getting off. She thinks of the shattered hopes hurtling away from the stations along with broken brick and debris. She thinks of all the dreams on board the *Titanic* all those years ago, sinking, same as the ones on the *Lusitania*, burbling down with the fine china, the rich and the poor crumpling on the ocean floor.

Lilly pulls her attention back to her son, now restless again.

Lilly thinks of Robert and Hugh, huddled under the kitchen table. She wonders if Robert has been saving the cream or if he pours without thinking. Her whole self, body and soul, wants out of this bed, home, both her boys beside her, so she can see them safe.

Sooner than she thinks, Lilly lies on the mattress with them, four now, counting the seconds that the bomb whistles, still airborne, harmless until the thud. She tries to gauge, by the volume of the thump, how close the bomb has struck. They pass the night under the table. Sirens sound again, urgent as her newborn's cry, each wailing out into the night, requiring response and response. There, in the dark, she feels her feeble infant against her breast.

She breathes in the feel of them together, and then she allows herself to count the fact that the Germans have been, more and more, saving a bomb or two, the way she saves the cream from the milk. The strongest blasts are held for London. More often, though, there's plenty left for railway junctions like Crewe. Lilly sees, there in the dark, that separating cream from milk is not enough to keep her children strong.

In the morning, after she sees Robert out to work, she begins to make her plans. *Is this how Davey did it? Sneaking off to meet the sergeant. And John, telling lies about his age so they'd take him.* He climbed out the window, following his big brother, pressing his fossil into her hand.

"For the bones of us, Lilly," he'd said. "So we can really live."

How small she'd felt, watching him go. Powerless, still young enough to believe he'd come home. John with his fossils. John and his honor and valor. Are those layers wrapped around him, preserved in death?

She pushes the idea from her head, pulls the baby closer to her; she takes a breath, looks up at the ceiling, above which Hugh still sleeps. She thinks of her mother, asking, time and again, to go out to work. She recalls the pinched face, the controlled dab of the napkin, the lowered eyes. Might Davey and John have been content to stay at home if Mummy had been able to provide for her children in the way she wanted?

On the night when the last arrangement has been made—a family found, the tickets booked—Lilly climbs the stairs, performs her ritual, checking on Hugh, brushing her teeth, then returning to her dressing table to rub in the tiny bit of face cream she has hoarded, and brush her hair. She slides into bed beside Robert. His breathing is slow and steady, but he isn't yet snoring. She places her hand on his shoulder.

"Robert," she whispers. "We're going."

He rolls over, meets her eyes.

"You're safe with me."

She feels the doubt rise again. She doesn't want it—doesn't want to doubt her own husband's capability. A second doubt rises beside it—this one is of herself. Is this what Mummy felt? Why she didn't dare defy Daddy?

Lilly pushes it out of her way. She strokes Robert's shoulder.

"Safe enough," he says. It's almost a question.

"Ah, Robert, even you can't fend off the German Army over our heads." She draws herself to him, unbuttons his pajama top, breathes in the feel of skin against skin.

Hugh takes the steps onto the train ahead of her as though this is a holiday he's going on, to Betws-y-Coed, a village in a sheltered valley in Wales whose name means prayer house in the woods. Lilly and the boys will share a house with a family, live on a farm. Lilly knows neither the family nor how long they will stay. She climbs on behind Hugh, wee Robby in her arms. Without looking back, she knows Robert is striding about the platform, searching for someone to whom he can speak. She wishes he wouldn't, wishes they could get on quietly like the other women and children. Lilly watches him, eyes a little too bright, cheeks flushed.

She hears him tell the porter he's a British Railway man, to watch out for her. She feels her own flush rise. She can take care of them. She recalls her father's anger, his need to do it all, her mother's silenced wants. She steps toward Robert, stands on tiptoes to kiss his cheek. "We're all right, Robert," she says. She lets him settle them in the compartment, hoping this helps him. As the train pulls away from the platform, she imagines herself and the boys flowing away from Robert, separating as easily as the cream slides out of the milk bottle, to keep the family strong, but as Robert and the station disappear from Lilly's sight, and as the train rolls into the countryside, Lilly thinks of her brothers, believing they could sail away and be something more. She recalls the sinking of the unsinkable, the Lusitania, her own brothers sinking down, her mother and father in the ground together, hardening. Layers of years pour off as the train thwacks on, herself and these two boys, her past, present and future all here in the compartment with her. Daddy said not to dwell in the past. Still, she can't push away the thought of the earth going down and down, of John digging it all up, hoarding it under his bed.

On the farm she's going to, will she and Hugh be asked to dig? The soft earth, the recent layer of detritus, yields food. Dig deeper, to the hard layers below. Doesn't that hard past, too, support them against this time, this war, as though the molten center of humanity has erupted. Lilly wants it all packed back down, cooled by the seas; she imagines craters filling in with soft soil. Robby sleeps in her arms. Hugh faces the window; she looks around him and discovers that he isn't watching but dozing instead. She gathers him to her, holds her spine straight as the train rattles west.

"For the bones of us," her brother said. "So we can really live."

Chickens peck randomly, greeting them on the path that leads to the farmhouse door. Mummy said chickens were filthy.

Weren't the eggs good, though, and a necessary part of a big breakfast for the boys? The luxury of an extra egg for a cake. Lilly stands at the kitchen door, Robby in one arm, suitcase in the other, no hand left to hold Hugh properly. They make do with Hugh holding the top of her hand that holds the case. Would her brothers have been that good at that age? Did Mummy ever hold their hands? There is no one to ask now.

Lilly expects a large woman to come to the door. Mrs. Thomas, Farmer Thomas' wife. She wonders what they will be expected to do to earn their keep.

A light breeze ruffles the baby's blanket. A border collie trots up from behind, tail wagging, followed by a woman of Lilly's own diminutive height, wiping dirt-encrusted hands on her apron. She extends her hand. Lilly sets down the suitcase, feels the woman's warm hand in hers.

Once more, the years draw down, under a bright sky, into this pinpoint of time. With her now are John's fossil in her hand, his one leg already out the window, her father's fists on the table, her mother's silent resignation. All of them now fossils of the heart, the bones of them within her and within her sons.

Mrs. Thomas' hand in hers somehow stanches the long-felt ache for her mother's. It's Lilly's turn now, and she knows as surely as she knows her feet are firmly planted on this earth that she's done what her mother never could. She's linked hands not just with this stranger but with the thousands of women who make up their own kind of army to fight this war: the Women's Voluntary Service, tending women and children, seeing them safe.

Mrs. Thomas lifts Lilly's case, and, as they turn to go inside, Lilly sends up a silent whisper to her brother. "For the bones of us, John. This time, we'll live."

Nesting Doll

As the elephants amble into the ring, a pain comes, harder than the ones before it—almost too hard to ignore. Jennie focuses on the elephants' bejeweled headdresses—embellishments that make her think of fat ballerinas—as the tightness wraps around her middle. When it releases, she notices the girl standing on the back of the lead elephant. Her size seems wrong, fairylike. Jennie nicknames her Tinkerbell, then submerges her hand in the bag of buttery popcorn as the animals and their fairy leader make their way around the ring.

The elephants stop at the front, and, one after the other, balance on little round tubs, each with its front legs on the rump of the elephant ahead. The animal in front squeezes all four feet onto the little tub; Tinkerbell balances on top, the smallest ballerina on top of the largest ballerina. The others remind Jennie of a set of nesting dolls. Jennie has begun to feel a little like a nesting doll herself. She has begun to feel like the big, ugly outermost one.

When she was a girl, in the first trailer she remembers, still living with her mother and father and sister, she owned an almost-complete set of nesting dolls. She had found them at the flea market when she ran ahead while her mother haggled over tube socks. The old lady at the stall pulled them apart to show her. The top half of the biggest one was missing, as well as the third. Still, the lady pulled them out—smaller, smaller, smaller, until she reached the smallest one.

"This one," the lady said, "is the only one carved from one whole, solid piece of wood." She placed the doll in Jennie's hand, the cool, smooth wood taking up nearly her whole palm.

Jennie begged her mother for them, jumping up and down. Her mother shook her head and moved on, stopping three stalls down, captivated by waffle irons and toasters.

"*Matryoshka*," the seller said. She folded Jennie's palm around the tiny doll and handed the rest to her.

At night, Jennie placed the dolls on the windowsill beside her bed. Soon she lost the bottom half of the second doll. When the 3:10 train rolled by in the dark, the top of the doll rocked, perched in what should have been the fourth doll, but was now the third.

Only months after the old lady pressed the doll into Jennie's hand, she handed the fourth doll to her sister, seventeen years old—eleven years older than she. The September night chill slid in when Lauren slid up the window as the rumble of the train began and slid her body through the slit in the broken screen. The top of the second doll, then perched on top of the smallest, rocked harder. Jennie pulled them in with her, pulled up the threadbare, graying sheet, curled on her side, waited for her mother to come in the morning and find Lauren gone; Momma sat on the floor beside the bed, rocking and glaring, whispering, "Why didn't you stop her?"

Jennie's mother didn't move while Jennie dressed and hurried into the kitchen, pulled a Pop-Tart from the box and ran, then, to the bus stop, red clay kicking up into the pines, dolls bouncing in her hand-me-down fairy princess book bag. Daddy said he would whittle a new set, paint them like Americans.

In the back of her dresser drawer, Jennie still has the bottom half of that big nesting doll and the very smallest one, the one that is made from one whole, solid piece of wood.

Jennie thinks of it as she watches the Tinkerbell matryoshka, standing now, beside the lead elephant. The elephant lifts a peanut, feeds herself; the elephant lifts a peanut, feeds the girl. A fresh pain grips Jennie. She begins to perspire, there next to her sister, not a sister at all, but so-called because she moved in the year after Lauren left, her father taking the space Jennie's own father had left. Nina, sliding into Lauren's bed.

They moved soon after, closer to Nina's grandparents, away from the red clay and rolling hills at the top of South Carolina to the sandy swampland between the midlands and the coast. They piled what they could into the bed of Ralph's faded green pickup: her mother's kitchen things, their clothes, mattresses, TV, not much else. The only thing of her father's to come with them had been his workbench, sturdy and well used, and which he'd made himself.

Jennie fans herself with the program, watches the tails swish, feels slightly dizzy. She scans the list of acts. How much longer? Have they seen the acrobats? Lions? Horses? She grips the armrests. For the first time ever, she shakes her head when Nina offers cotton candy.

The spring after they moved, just beyond the long grass that grew at the edges of the new-to-them trailer, lying in the cool sand underneath, Jennie found a turtle. The day was unseasonably warm. She wore last year's shorts and T-shirt, the waistbands not quite meeting. These were the last of the clothes Daddy bought for her, before the yelling got louder even than the rumble of the train in the night, and then the slap of the screen door, the roar of his truck. Momma yelled into the night after the sounds of him quieted, "You never did love her like she was yours." How many weeks was it until Ralph's truck first rumbled up the path? And how many weeks between that and the morning Jennie watched the red clay puff into little clouds behind them as they pulled away, driving to the trailer further south?

Alone as usual, outside that trailer, Jennie's clear blue eye met the orange of the turtle's for the merest flash before the animal drew into its shell, closing up firmly. She crawled into the cool dark under the trailer, lifted the creature onto her lap and traced the outline of the panels of its shell. After she drew her finger over each panel, she rested one hand in the sandy ground beside her and sat as still as she could manage. The sun began to lower and the air under the trailer took on a chill when the animal poked out its head. Slowly, gently, she lifted it. She tiptoed past her mother, who had come out, at last, from her room, her face taking on new shadows in front of the TV. Jennie tucked the animal into a battered shoe box in the back of her closet.

In the morning, she stole her mother's phone from the kitchen counter, took a picture and tucked the phone in her book bag. Her mother became frantic, checking in the kitchen, flinging back couch cushions, scratching through her large bag in search of the phone. Jennie hurried out to wait for the bus at the end of the long, rutted drive. She held her book bag on her lap to keep the phone safe, hoped for a moment alone with her teacher so she could show her the image.

"Terapene Carolina, subspecies t. Carolina," Mrs. Thomason said. Jennie squinted. Mrs. Thomason patted her on the head. "Carolina box turtle. See the short tail? It's hard to tell, but this one is probably a girl. When you get home, look on the bottom of her shell. She has a hinged plastron—can you say plastron, Jennie?"

"Plastron," Jennie repeated.

"These are the only turtles in the world that can close their shells all the way. The plastron—it's like an attic door—is how they do it."

Other students began to come in. Mrs. Thomason told Jennie to put away her phone. Jennie nodded, did as she was told. Later, just before recess, Mrs. Thomason allowed her to go to the library, a special trip to get a book about turtles. At the end of the day, Mrs. Thomason told her to take good care of the turtle. "Don't let anyone move it far."

In the afternoon, in the trailer, just her and the remaining nesting dolls, Jennie balanced the turtle on one leg and the book on the other. Her new sister-not-sister went to a different school, a middle school, with afterschool activities. Momma worked a second shift at the 7-Eleven, now open 24-7. Jennie didn't know what kind of work Ralph did.

She brought the turtle grass, and lettuce and carrots she had tucked away at lunch. This lasted for seven days, until she came home and found the turtle and two eggs in the shoebox. The next morning, the turtle was gone. The eggs, like miniature versions of peeled, boiled eggs—the kind for eating—rested in the center of the box. She wrapped them in toilet paper and carried them to school. There was always someone with Mrs. Thomason. In the afternoon, at home, Jennie set them on the windowsill, thinking to keep them warm and help them hatch. She pulled down the blind so Nina wouldn't see. By the time she checked on them the next afternoon, they had crumpled in on themselves. Jennie stood, staring, not able to make herself touch them. She pulled the blind back over them, felt glad to be in the den in front of her mother when Nina screamed. She followed behind, hoping to be unnoticed when her mother and Ralph responded. She watched Ralph lift the dead eggs. He extended his arm so the eggs came right up to her face as he passed, but he said nothing, only walked out the front door and to the edge of the woods, where he tossed the eggs.

A bead of sweat meanders down Jennie's spine as the last of the last elephant disappears behind the curtain. The crowd applauds. Jennie feels her own clapping is in slow motion, even though she can see that her rhythm fits. She inhales, deeply. The clowns are out now. Below her, a woman cackles.

On Nina's other side, hard-jawed and chewing tobacco, spit cup between his legs, Nina's boyfriend. On his other side, his son and their small daughter, born the second time they lived together. They have come together and pulled apart so may times Jennie now thinks of their relationship as accordion music, expanding and contracting, taking deep, yawning breaths that are filled with open air and, in Nina's case, weeping. Then the compression of them back together, the compression of Nina.

How many times has Jennie happened on them over the few years they have been in and out of together? She has glimpsed Nina's back against the brick wall behind The Cotton Bottom, Nina scrunched in the bed of the truck. Always, Dayton seems to be pressing too hard, crushing in. Once upon a time, Jennie thought she had found something better for herself.

Out of the corner of her eye, Jennie watches Dayton bend toward his cup, spit, reminding her of Ralph, of his chaw cup in the cup holder that hangs from the door of his ancient truck, 1970-something, stick-on-the-column, faded green.

The first time she was alone with Ralph in the truck was years after they moved. Eighth grade. She noticed that the boys had started noticing her budding breasts. Last year's jeans, a little too short and tight, didn't help matters. Kyle Leavitt sat two rows away from her, had a habit of leaning forward, head on his stack of books. Kyle's books alternated between being a pillow, a viewing stand on which to rest his head and leer, or a weight enough for him to demonstrate the cut of his muscles as he walked down the hall, T-shirt a size too small, the sleeves clutching his biceps, arms bent at just the right angle for maximum bulge. In the bathroom, some of the girls tittered at the notion of him stuffing his pants the way they wore two and three bras. Jennie steered clear of the lot of them.

That year, a January morning in the classroom, Kyle leering as usual, a sharp winter sun slicing through the window, Mrs. Patten directed a C-team football player to lower the blinds. Mrs. Patten turned off the lights. For a moment, in almost total darkness, Jennie relaxed. No one's eyes could be on her.

The projector whirred to life. Mrs. Patten didn't pull down the screen.

"Look up," she said.

Eyes adjusting to the semi-dark, Jennie made out that Mrs. Patten had used a stack of books in a similar manner to Kyle, as a stand and stabilizer to turn the projector on its side and beam its images onto the ceiling.

"Andromeda," Mrs. Patten said. "We will begin to study the stars here, in ELA, as well as in science. Here, we will also study the stories that accompany some of the constellations. You will create your own constellation and story at the end of this unit of study."

They learned stories of Orion the Hunter, of Andromeda, of Cassiopeia, Perseus, of love and vanity and retribution, of fighting and death, of myth and truth. They learned which of the constellations rose in their own sky each night.

Perseus was visible the night Momma went to the hospital.

"Getting her woman parts taken," Nina whispered in the dark.

Before Momma came home, Ralph took Nina to stay with his people, just until Momma got better.

Later, Ralph stood in the den, glanced at her mother on the sofa, freshly back from the hospital, pale cheeks against the blue cushions, dark circles under her closed eyes, her body curled into itself. Ralph looked Jennie over from the tips of her sandals, chipped pink nail polish on her toes, to her smoothly shaven legs, a new thing, and on up to the slight gap between her jeans and her T-shirt, hesitating at the cross that bridged the gap between her budding breasts and pale throat. Jennie thought first of Kyle, leering, and then of her own father; she wondered if he had people, if she could be sent to stay with them.

Ralph looked her in the eye. He nodded. "You come on with me in the morning," he said.

"Momma might need me."

He raised an eyebrow. "Your momma needs to get herself healed."

High in the cab, 3:23 blinking on the dash clock, Jennie thought of her mother, cut in the middle, hollowed out. Ralph rolled down the window. The November air made Jennie pull her knees to her chest, curl against the door, the smell of cigarettes and peach cigarillos embedded in the vinyl of the bench seat. They bumped down the dark road, moving toward the dark waters where Ralph once took her and Nina, hooking catfish on a hot July afternoon.

They pulled up near nothing, parked under one of many live oaks. He stepped to the middle of the rutted road, swung his head back. A shooting star flashed. She pointed. "Make a wish," she whispered.

"Ain't nothing but a bunch of rocks in the sky."

He drew on his cigarette, and on the exhale told her his momma did stuff like that—wished on stars. He said she used to sit on the porch, pull him onto her knee when he was little, and tell him about all the people in the sky. He snorted.

"Only one I remember is the hunter."

He lifted the bow and rifle from the rack. "Either sex today." His teeth flashed in the dark. Jennie took a minute to recall that either sex meant he could take a male or female deer, or both. He slung his weapons over his shoulder, put one hand on her shoulder, pressed down, hard. "Not a peep from now on." He leaned down and held his face inches from hers. "You understand?"

She nodded.

"You do good this time, I might bring you again."

When they reached the blind, built several feet in the air around a live oak, he stopped and nudged her ahead. The Spanish moss swayed in the breeze, half moon in and out of the clouds as she felt rung to rung into the dark branches. She knew it was called a blind because the deer wouldn't see them, but in the dark, hands and feet on splintery wood rungs, she was the blind one. Ralph pressed his hand against her butt, hurrying her.

On the platform, she knelt on the floor of the blind and looked out through a small, paneless window while Ralph checked the sights on the rifle and bow. Her knees numbed quickly. She shifted to her backside. Ralph grabbed her elbow, pulled her back up. He nodded, indicating she should watch.

In the pre-dawn, cramped in the hunting blind, knees bent and aching already, hands slid between thighs for warmth and still nearly numb, her hip the only warm spot, pressed against Ralph's lean leg. His arms, strong and ropy, all but his jutting gut giving the sense of the Marine he had been. Just the one tour, in peacetime. (Could you really call it a tour? She had once heard Momma hiss this during an argument, late at night.)

She thought of her mother again as the red sun lifted, steam rising from the swamp, a small doe stepping into sight; Ralph rose, stealthy except for the slight jiggle of white flesh. He had the animal down before the click and swish of the arrow registered. Ralph climbed down from the stand. Jennie followed, stood beside him over the doe. She thought of her mother, hollow; she thought of herself, having nested in that now-hollow place, in that safe place beyond memory, as Ralph directed her to grab the animal, help drag it to the truck. He lay the animal down, blood crusting her brown fur around the entry wound, dark eye wide in the bed of the truck, the click of the tailgate shutting. Ralph's hands landed, then, on Jennie's shoulders, turning her. The metal ridges of the letters F-O-R-D dug in. Sweat in the November dawn. Light. Hollow, hollow, hollow.

Ralph dressed the deer in the shed on the workbench that used to be her father's, on which her father built her toddler chair and then her swingset, left at the old place. In the night, Jennie tiptoed from her room, climbed onto the flat of the bench, still slightly damp. She lay her head where her father used to place his hands, where the doe lay that afternoon. She settled her hand on the wood. Dark blood had already sealed over the pale surface, mottled the bench's legs. Eyes closed, she imagined a shadow of her father over her, hands sliding under her, lifting, come to claim her.

Four tigers prowl into the ring. The tamer struts past them, tiger-stripe jacket unzipped, exposing the edges of too-dark six-pack abs. His white teeth, horsey rectangles, gleam as he cracks the whip. Jennie tightens her grip on the armrests, breathes into the next pain. She thinks of Michael, of the morning she met him.

She heard the familiar rumble of Ralph's truck down the ruts that served as a driveway, too early, and followed by the sharp slap of the door closing. She heard the crackle of another set of tires over dried leaves just before dawn, in the middle of hunting season a couple of years after that time with Ralph in the blind.

Jennie parted the blinds on her window, watched the boy, not much older than she, slide out of his own truck. He hesitated, noticed her there in the gap, nodded and smiled a perfect smile, there in the pre-dawn halflight.

While they dressed their deer, she pulled on her best dress, an out-of-season seersucker that held her tightly, perfectly, at the waist. In the kitchen she brewed coffee, which she carried to them, dark and steamy. She sat beside them in fraying aluminum folding chairs at the edge of the trailer, arms crossed and hands tucked into her armpits for warmth while they sipped.

Sometime after the sun was full, Michael stood, handed her his empty coffee mug, his fingers lingering around hers, and turned for his truck. She hadn't been introduced, just learned his name when Ralph said it. She watched him pull out, her hands trying to gather leftover warmth. Water oak and hickory leaves kicked out from under his tires. He raised his right hand, gave one quick flick of a wave. She noticed, too, the half turn of his head in the rear window of the cab, framed by the antler sticker and the NRA one.

Two months later, he graduated high school. He invited her to the blind to celebrate, just the two of them and a bottle of homebrew a friend of his made, clear in the moonlight and burning its way through her insides, a preparation. In the predawn, under the bare bulb outside the front door of the trailer, he handed her a single bloom, broken from the tall stalk of a golden canna. She twirled it in her hand, watching him bump down the ruts.

Only then did she notice the ribbon sticker on his tailgate, like the ones that say *Support our troops* or *Save the ta-tas*, only his said *I Support Pussy.* Perhaps it had been on there when he bought the truck, second-hand.

Within a month, he was packing for basic training. The week before he left, they went to the blind in the wee hours of every morning, Michael on his knees on top of her, and then on his knees with his eyes on the scope, a perfect shot every time.

When he pulled back down the rutted drive after basic training, he had added a *Support our Troops* ribbon to the opposite side of the tailgate from the pussy one. Soon he would add extra training and the pay that went with it. When he received his notice of deployment, Jennie's mother signed the license so Jennie could be married as a minor. Jennie took a job, third shift, at the 7-Eleven. She imagined moving out and away.

After his tour, Michael rented them a single-wide in the same park, near Momma and Ralph. Each night he lined up his weapons—guns, knives, and scopes—on the card table in the kitchen. He took them apart and cleaned them with Ralph sitting beside him, watching, more nights than not. Ralph sipped his Bud Light. He had taken to buying the big bottles by then, so he wouldn't have to go to the fridge so often; even when she was home, Momma was too tired to do much but sleep between her shifts. Michael's glass of tequila rested on the shelf to his left. His eyes seemed smaller, as though they had shrunk to fit the smallest scope, become part of the laser that led from him to death. He had earned the job of sniper.

The second Friday back, after supper, he and Ralph huddled over the table, as usual. Michael lifted a scope, paused, set it back down, and assembled a gun, black barrel gleaming. She heard the click behind her as she did the dishes, the sound now familiar but still disconcerting. Steam from the soapy water rose, good for the skin, her sister used to say, her real sister. Opens up your pores. Lets out all the dirt.

The scope made a swishing sound as he attached it.

"I've got you in my sight," he said.

She placed a dish in the drainer. She sunk her hand into the water.

"Turn around."

She stilled, hand under the hot liquid.

"Turn around."

She rotated slowly, like a doll on a music box. She stood, hands dripping sudsy water. The gun was aimed at her forehead. She imagined she could feel the red dot of the laser in the middle, like one of those Indian women they studied in school, the red dot a mark, meaning what, she couldn't remember; instead, she recalled the first doe, the blood crusting around the entry wound.

Michael laughed.

Ralph laughed.

Michael lowered the scope.

"You never hear the sound of the one that kills you," he said.

Jennie turned back to the dishes, finished washing, drying, putting away. She tiptoed to her room, their room, dug to the back of the drawer, pulled out her Swiss army knife. She placed it under her pillow. In the morning, she moved it to her purse. She began to keep it with her at all times, sometimes sliding it into her pants pocket, taking it even for quick trips to the bathroom.

Michael began to find her in his sights at different times of day: from his chair in front of the trailer when she came back from work or when she stepped out of the shower, still dripping. She wished, then, for her knife; she wished for a way to cut herself loose.

Michael began to add stickers to the truck, mostly logos for gun and scope manufacturers that came with things he bought on the Internet. He placed them around the existing stickers. He made his continued support for the troops obvious by wearing camo, polishing his weapons; he made his continued support for pussy obvious by waking her often in the day, saying nothing as he pressed in and in. She tried to close her eyes against the slice of sun through the gap in the blinds. She heard he spent the nights, when she worked, showing his support in the parking lots of various bars in the county.

At the start of the new year, he signed up for a second tour. He left just after her 18th birthday. She is a Pisces, the fish. She took herself to the edge of the swamp two weeks after. There, alone in the shelter of the trees, she unwrapped the Clearblue Easy package, squatted, then watched for the blue that says, "positive."

She thought of Michael's scope. She thought of Ralph and Nina and their people. She thought of her father, wondered again if he had people. She told no one.

When she secreted away one morning to Columbia, a thin roll of twenties tucked down her sock, she discovered she was too late, past the thirteen-week-abortion limit in South Carolina. She could go to Georgia, the lady said. Each week, though, the cost increased more than Jennie's paycheck could match.

The horses come next, prancing, blue-feathered headdresses rising from their manes, necks curled and heads pointing down. She hangs her own head, trying to breathe deeply and quietly. When she looks up again, the whole circus is in the ring—elephants, horses, a llama, the acrobats, clowns. Jennie presses up from her seat. Up the stairs, toward the red exit sign, she climbs. She makes the hall, hears the crack of some trainer's whip, faint now, behind her. The hall is wide, empty, a concrete ring around the building. She thinks of it, the circle of the building, brick and glass, this exterior ring of concrete and cinder block, the circles of seats angling down to the center, to the flat, smaller circle where the whole circus now gathers.

She leans against the cool concrete, presses her head against it. She rests there, between pains. After the next one, she pushes off, turns for the restroom. She can't see a sign. It doesn't matter, though, which way she goes, she will come on it eventually. Isn't that the beauty of the circle? Inside, in the stall, carefully bolted, she sits, braces her hands against each wall, and lowers her head against an ad for next month's monster truck rally. The next pain makes her feel she may break, right across her pelvis, two halves of her falling away.

She sweats. She expands. She gives in, lets go of the stall walls, folds over herself. She does not know how long she is there, only that someone comes, banging on the stall door. Her mother, she thinks, only that can't be right. Momma is at work, or else asleep.

"You okay?"

"Yes ma'am." She stands. So much dark blood below. She sits again. The pains subside. The roar of the crowd rises once more, then falls. She waits for people to come and go. Nina comes.

"Jennie? You in there?"

She hears herself say she's fine. They should go on. She will get herself home. She drove herself there, after all.

Outside, November air bites at the sweaty places, a thousand needles jabbing at her. Headlights swim. A man takes her arm, pulls her back from the edge of the sidewalk. "Watch yourself there, darlin'."

She wanders lot to lot before she finds her car, now the only one in the remote lot. She slides in, leaves the door open, reclines the seat, breathes through another spasm, weaker than the ones that came before. She lifts her phone, sets it back down. She pulls the door closed, rolls down the window. The sky is cloudless, the moon a sliver, a few stars visible. She makes out Orion's belt. Somewhere under this same sky, her father may still live. Lauren too. Somewhere, under a far-off version of this sky, Michael lies on some bunk or bed, perhaps with another woman, perhaps with a gun. Neither Lauren nor her father will come for her. Too soon, Michael will.

Jennie pulls the seat upright, cranks the car. The tank is full. She has heard of a place a few miles beyond the county line, a sandhill called Pack's Bluff. It is rumored to be so dark there that you can see the whole night sky. If she can make the Bluff, she will perhaps see Cassiopeia. Maybe Perseus will stand, high in the sky, or else there will be other constellations, whose names she does not need to know, pointing the way.

As Jennie pulls the gearshift down to drive, she recalls Mrs. Thomason hunched over the stolen phone; she recalls her voice telling about box turtles. She remembers the book Mrs. Thomason gave to help her understand, the texture of the page under her fingers, the letters revealing sentences that said if the turtle is moved more than half a mile from its territory, it may never find its way back but spend years unsystematically searching; that said that turtles abandon their young; that they close up completely in the face of an attack, offering only their hard carapace to predators.

The book said that even if they are severely damaged, turtles can regenerate their shells.

Clear Blue Line

I do not know if I will marry the baby's father; do not know officially, medically, that he is to be called father and I mother. I have felt, for weeks now, something tiny but sure, a shift that says something within me has changed. While I wait, I turn my back on the slim white piece of plastic that will, in less than three minutes, make its silent pronouncement regarding parenthood. Through the thick glass in the upstairs bathroom window, I can see the gray-blue water of the Firth of Clyde. This, the estuary of the River Clyde, is a wavery band of salty water that stretches from the pebbly Ayrshire shore to the Wee Cumbrae, Arran and the other southernmost western isles. Water runs behind me, clear, from tap to sink, making sounds that imply that my actions are the same this morning as any other. From downstairs, Granny calls to tell me that breakfast is ready.

I have come home, here to my Granny and Papa's house, a few towns over from the town in which I grew up. I have come for my holidays, on semester break from university in South Carolina. The tickets for this trip were booked six months ago, my passport renewed, letters written back and forth to Papa about what hikes we might take together, the two of us. We could not have predicted that it would be here that time would ripen the seed in me just enough to register.

Seconds tick over on my watch. The water outside goes about its normal daily ebb and flow, lapping up on cloud-shrouded humps of land.

"Just a minute," I call back down. I am supposed to be on time, to take my chair at the red Formica-topped table in the kitchen and eat Scots Porridge Oats with my Papa while my slim Irish Granny eats her ration of half a grapefruit, sliced the night before when she put the oats in to soak. I will sit between them, linking the three of us in this ritual.

I look at my watch. I'll be down in closer to two minutes, actually. The package said Clearblue Easy, after all, not Clearblue Instantly. I bought it in Glasgow, afraid to get it in the chemist in Largs, the village in which I have visited my grandparents since my parents brought me home from the adoption agency.

I have promised myself not to look until the time is up, so I focus again on the line of ocean outside; think of the beginning of the Clyde, in the middle of Scotland; think of her flowing out from Scotland's waist, becoming wider and wider like a woman opening herself to the world. I wonder about my own birth mother; try to imagine us for a moment, standing back-to-back. She must have been almost exactly my age when she stood, looking out of some window onto the Firth of Forth, the body of water that digs into Scotland's east coast, forming the other curve of her waist. I have counted the weeks; know that this child, now too small to be counted in any way other than a thin line on a plastic pregnancy test, will be due on almost the same day as I. Like me, this child has come unbidden. We each, in a time no one chose, swam in and made a connection as sure as salmon who swim home generation after generation.

I think about how, in Celtic myth, salmon are the symbol for knowledge. Where these fish swim, some truth is revealed. I wonder if my birth mother knew, as I do, before some science said so. I wonder if she felt the shift, the knowing, before even her period was late. I think of her as a real salmon, changing from the bright pink of her youth to a darker, more brooding shade that came on with the offspring within her. I think of her as salmon, swimming back out, having deposited the next generation. I think of her swimming out to catch the tide in the place where the Forth meets the Gaelic Sea. I think of her taking the knowledge with her.

I turn to the sink, hear my Papa's voice, now urgent with the threat of breakfast. His words boom from the kitchen, easily rising and curving up the stairs to the opposite end of the house. My Papa's voice booms easily around most curves, reaching the opposite end of wherever he is. It is almost impossible to escape.

I do not need to ponder the Clearblue line when I see it, there on the edge of the sink, undeniable as my Papa's voice below or the Clyde outside.

"Coming," I call back down, hiding the evidence easily on the way.

Together we descend, this child and I. We come to breakfast, to a ritual I have lived my whole life. I come with a new knowledge, sit at the table for the first time with the beginnings of a person to whom I am linked, not by porridge and hikes, but by limb and life, bone and blood.

I do not know if I will marry this child's father. I do not know to what color this child will change me as I shed my girlhood pink. I know that I will carry him with me down to the edge of the River Clyde; that we will fly together over the deep, deep firth and thousands of miles across the sea to make our own home. I do not know all the things I will need to. I think we can begin by learning each other.

Understory

I

Beneath

Her hand, pale and plump, rubs clean one small arc of the floor. The yellow core of the wood hides under dark stain, decades of footfalls, spills from tenant after tenant, and now, layers of unswept grime. *Sapwood.* She extends her reach. *Insides of trees.* She rubs in a circle now. *Pine.* Shortleaf, most likely, same as the ones that grew on her granddaddy's homeplace. *Pinus echinata*, with its two-inch needles, dimpled bark, tiny holes where the resin crept out, making it sticky to the touch. In those thick woods, she'd lain her hand on all the trees. Hadn't she had a little book with all their names? Hadn't she known them according to their rough feel against her smooth skin: red maple, sassafras, wax myrtle, winged elm, box elder, sycamore, loblolly pine and her favorite, shagbark hickory?

She had scurried out, touching them, calling their names when the men came to fell them, to strip the land and reveal the red clay beneath, to strip each limb and expose the smooth, pale insides. Some, she knew, would be placed back upright, stained but still standing tall as God intended, utility poles the new name for them. Others were ground and soaked and turned to pulp, then paper, which would be used and discarded after it served its purpose. The rest would be sliced into thin strips of floor like the one beneath her.

She opens her eyes now, continues to rub. The room is bare except for her bag, bright yellow faux leather, and a clipboard she stole, from McDonald's, she thinks. With her other hand, she fingers a note scrawled on a torn strip of paper. Her thumb worries the frayed edge. She found it last night, perhaps, or the night before, lying in the middle of the floor where the card table had been, where she now lies. She recalls setting out in the bright morning, leaving her baby girl, Clara, with Bobby, Clara's father. She can't recall now what it was she left to do, knows only she came home after dark, found the note on the bare wood, saying he was gone. Clara too.

She closes her eyes again, sniffs the floor. *Chicory.* She often smells chicory on floors, in the air, even in the middle of the city, despite cars and trucks rolling past spewing diesel. She recalls following her daddy into the woods one July Saturday, when there still were woods. She was small enough then to hide behind a hickory and she watched as he grasped one stalk of chicory then another. Their delicate blue petals shook as he hauled them out of the ground, red clay clinging to the hairy roots. She shivered after each one, scuttled back to the kitchen ahead of him, waited in the chair by the kitchen table, feet dangling, white blonde hairs on her arms standing on end. She heard the rush of water and knew he was washing the roots outside under the pipe. When he brought them in, they dripped across the floor, pale red dots from door to oven. After he baked them, he wrapped his broad hands around the white mortar and pestle and ground the dark roots, body of the land. He poured boiling water over them in the morning, not even bothering to sit while he drank, in the dark by the sink.

Blood of the land, he called it.

By the next July, the one when they came for the trees, Daddy was gone. She thought of him as she watched the trucks roll over that year's blue blossoms. She thought of how he hurried out one dark winter night. "Nothing worth harvesting here. Not for me. Not anymore." She suspected he meant something she didn't understand when Momma grabbed the mortar. She recalls the mortar, sailing white through the dark doorway after him. Momma collapsed to the floor then, not caring that her yellow skirt lay against the spilled dark chicory, allowing a permanent stain to seep in.

Didn't she sit next to Momma, rub her hands in the chicory, lift it to her face, breathe?

She breathes now, tries to remember. She recalls going to the kitchen, finding the empty Budweiser tall boys on the kitchen counter. They towered over a dark plastic vial and several used jars of toddler food, green and orange puree residue clinging around the rims. She lifted the vial, shook, found it empty. When was the last time she took one? She ran a finger around the empty jar of carrot puree, put her finger to her lips, sucked, and imagined it was Clara's soft lips around her finger. Did she go to the sink then? Or was it later? No matter. When she went, she turned the tap. The water was gone too. She lay down then, to think.

Now it is morning. The next morning or the next after that, she thinks.

II
Above

She stares at the roof, thinks of roofs over her head, of Granddaddy's roof, which had been his daddy's before that, how it was built by hand, slightly tilted against the rise of land on which it sat, the woods all around it. She remembers the rafters, splintering while she and Momma watched when the bulldozer came. It barely had to nudge the house to fell it. That was after Daddy left, and Momma couldn't keep it up. She sold the trees first, then the land itself before the first hard frost. That little tilted house wouldn't seem right next to those that would come in the new development.

Next, Aunt Ruth's roof over her head, too close in the hot attic and Uncle Earl's with the leak in the kitchen after that. Uncle Earl was not really an uncle at all, and the first in a series. The only roof to count on after Granddaddy's was the Sunday one in Grace Freewill Baptist. White clapboard outside, raw pine within, bare cross below the exposed beams. The cross was like the one to which the Lord Jesus was nailed. *Praise the Lord.* Momma held one hand in the air and one hand on her head. The preacher used to put one hand on each of their heads, after the land sold, after the house fell, before and during and after each of the uncles.

In those moments, she thought she might be able to become a tree, to stretch her limbs above and above until they met the Christ looking down on them.

III

Within

She rolls onto her side, pushes herself up, sits. She brushes off her shirt, notices a stain. *Christ died to cleanse us.* She will find Bobby, she thinks, find her Clara, too.

Left, she goes, at the end of the ruts that stand for a driveway. Half a block, then onto the sidewalk by the four-lane. *Which way?* She chooses right, onto Cedar Lane Road, long, straight, unshaded. The sun reaches down, humidity thrusts in. She pushes back, footfall after footfall. Her bag bounces against her hip; her wallet lies, empty, within; one last scrap of paper clings to the black clipboard. She liked the feel of leaning on it when she filled out the application. She needed something solid to take home.

It is Friday, she thinks. Flags droop on doorsteps. Bunting sags on fences. Independence Day? Coming soon or gone? They were going to go to his momma's house, sit on the bare green lawn: fireworks, hot dogs, the wading pool in the back for Clara.

"Get some good cooking," Bobby had said.

When? Two nights ago? Three? Longer?

"Not like I get any here," he said. His face reddened. A vein on the back of his hand pulsed. He sipped his beer, rocked on his boots, sat, held out the empty. "Don't make me wait." His fist clenched, relaxed, clenched, occupied itself with the cool of the new beer. Seven left, sometimes enough.

She stops on a corner near the center of town, looks up, ignores the salty sweat that bites at the edges of her eyes. She ignores the men who brush past her, phones pressed to their cheeks. She can't remember which way to his mother's house. She presses forward, face reddening. Her bag bounces against her hip. Sweat rolls between her breasts and down the length of her spine and the backs of her legs.

On a corner she doesn't recognize, between buildings that rise taller than pine, she stops. A pair of women draw on cigarettes on the bench. A man stands beside them, laughing. The Legal Aid sign swings in front of her. She thinks she remembers coming somewhere like this with Momma. After which uncle? She thinks she remembers Momma saying, "Be a good girl and they'll give us what we need." Momma smoothed her skirt, smiled at the man across the desk.

She smoothes herself now, wraps her fingers around the handle, long metal. She pulls. The door is locked. She pulls again. She steps back.

"I need," she says. She says it aloud, there on the street, outside the locked door of the flatiron building at the intersection of Main and Elm. She searches for a sign. She pulls again. She needs to know which way to go. She shakes her head, hard. "You can't, you can't." She turns south on Main. She strides fast, bag on shoulder, clipboard solid in her arms where Clara should be. Clara, named after her mother. Clara, gone. Momma, gone.

"You can't take my baby." She walks hard and fast, her words matching her pace. She will find him. "You can't. Can not. Can not have. My baby. Can not take. What I need." She makes the end of the block.

She leans against the utility pole. Pale hands against wood, a splinter sliding in. Pine. Tall and strong. The kinds of pine: loblolly, longleaf, shortleaf. She turns skyward. The sun pierces her eyes. She neither squints nor lifts her hand to shade herself. Light slices in, bright and hot and beautiful. She is at the front of the church, hands stretching, barely reaching the solid pine just below the place where they nailed the feet of Christ. *Praise Jesus.* He has sent her here, she thinks. Here to the locked door, to the sun, the pine, the sky. She raises her hands to His infinity. *Hallelujah.* She feels Momma's hand, once again, on her head. She stretches skyward, jumps, jumps again.

"Praise Him." The words are in her, all around her. Who else has been in her, around her? Bobby—hard, burning. Clara—making her feel she might break then making her feel she might come together again. Who else has been within?

Christ has been waiting His turn, she thinks.

She casts off her shoes. She kneels. A small pebble digs in at her knee. The ground heats through her jeans. *Almost right.* She lies her body down, flat, stretches out her hands, stretches out her feet.

"Hallelujah."

Heat bears down on her back; heat rises, rises through her shirt. She rises, leaps, moves. Throws the clipboard, frees herself from the need for something solid. She lets the yellow straps fall from her shoulder into her hand. She flings that, too, into the street.

She walks away, fast. Utility pole pine and blooming crape myrtle saplings and stray people on benches look on.

"Jesus Christ is here."

A squat man stops her, grey cigarette dangling. "Ma'am. Ma'am. Ma'am." He tries to tell her to get her bag. Her ID, he says. She will need her ID.

She throws back her head.

"I know who I am." She reaches to the fractal light. "I am from there. I am of Him."

She moves on. *I need nothing.* She thinks of the bare wood floor, of the stripping of the pine to make it, of Christ, stripped on the cross.

She pulls away the shirt, drops it, keeps going.

Hallelujah.

Naked, in front of the fountain by the park, she leans back, raises arms.

"I am with Him." She pumps her arms, calls out again as she pulls off bra, jeans, all of it. "I am with Him."

A different man approaches. Then a woman, and another and another, the congregation making its way to the front of the church. She closes her eyes, waits for the feel of the preacher's hand on her.

Soon she feels hands against her back, on her arms, grasping, forcing her down, down, down, gritty grey on her shins and knees, digging little holes. Skin like the bark of the short pine. Blood oozing. *Raise the cup to your lips.* Hands pull her hands behind her back. Hands tie her feet. A sudden jolt, beginning at the base of her spine and rising through her. Her body courses with the charge. She is bound. A blanket over her. Lights all around, blue and white and red. More colors even than the names of trees, of God's creation. Yellow pine, yellow sun. Blue lights on the cars, blue flowers on the chicory. Concrete burns her belly. Wool scratches her back. She sweats. She bleeds. A figure comes forward, out of the white, red light flashing behind—blood of the land, blood of Christ. She feels herself lifted up.

Payline

James sits, hunched, on a bench between the arcade and the pebbled shore. Behind him, a gaggle of girls giggles out, their pitch in harmony with the tinkly music and sounds of one-armed bandits in play. Coins roll down the insides of the machines, become losers' money. James knows the fleeting thrill of the play, the pull on the arm, the delight as the columns whirl with hope, suspended overhead. He knows the clenching of the gut as the columns lower, lower, lower, then settle, one-two-three. If the game is lost, the player must decide if the risk is worth playing again.

James glances up the street, inland. He shifts his feet inside his black leather shoes. Does his jacket hide the coffee stain on his shirt? Grey-blue to match his eyes, Yves St. Laurent.

Largs is packed. It was the same on Cumbrae as he made his way to the ferry—loud children stuffing in ice creams, washing them down with Irn Brus. James can't fathom why it's like this on a Monday, but then James has never known the rhythm of children, the sway of school holidays. He thinks of this as he looks south down the firth; he thinks these swarms of children will make the woman he's waiting for harder to spot. They also camouflage him.

James wants to see her first no matter which way she comes—along the front toward him, from the ferry, from the top of the village; even if she comes from behind the arcade, she will have to cross the street in front of him. Alison. Her name whirls in his head. He has not yet tested it on his lips, felt it rise from his throat, vibrating, filling his mouth, then floating out from him into the world. This is what Alison did: came from him, unbidden, unknown, before she was taken away.

He'd thought it would be himself who would be away, forty-one years ago, when he came across the water and up the firth and in along the Clyde to Glasgow. He earned good marks in his course, gathered a girl by his side. The pair of them drank pints of heavy in the pubs, pointed to places on the map of the world that they might go when she was a fully qualified nurse and he an engineer. Less than a year it took them, to land in separate places, their baby settling with a couple on the other side of the country. Later, he landed a job at Hunterston, on the mainland, at least.

Even that is finished now, and himself tucked back into his dead parents' house while his daughter has been out in the world, away over Cumbrae and all Scotland's westernmost isles, right on to America, so her letter said. He's never known where her mother went.

He straightens his spine, there on the bench.

Any moment now, Alison will complete her journey back to him.

The village surges. James' belly rolls. His heart thumps. When was he last this aware? His skin tingles. James presses his hands on his thighs, pulls in his belly.

He recalls his own father, decades ago, outside the arcade, a special Saturday when they'd gone the opposite direction of the Glaswegians. He recalls his father's callused fingers pressing coins into James' small, smooth-skinned hand. He recalls the cigarette-rough of the old man's voice, saying, "That's all you get."

"Hold your winnings," he said. "Only fools go in again."

James could rise now, slip away. He smoothes his trousers, presses back his shoulders.

He sees her, striding down from the top of the village, auburn hair flowing behind her like a wake. The village stills. Everything falls away—the girls giggling, the ferry churning, the slot machines twirling.

James watches her pass on the opposite side of the street, stands to move to her, the moment suspended. *Alison.*

James steps across the street. Alison has stopped. She turns.

James stops, inches from her, this girl, this woman, his daughter.

"Alison." James leans, hand extended, waiting for her hand to land in his.

Where the Crust Breaks

The lock is reluctant. The key slid in nicely, but turning it isn't such a treat until she remembers the routine: a slight tug back out, a gentle jiggle and then the release. *Christ.* All this time and he did nothing about it. She hangs her head, wavy hair falling in front of her eyes, the one grey streak almost at dead center. She hesitates. The smallest nudge and she'll be in. First time in twenty-three years.

The grandfather clock punctuates the silence. Someone has been into wind, then, to make the house still seem alive. She nods. The solicitor, maybe. The neighbor who gave her the key. Taxi driver. Barman. She can't recall their names.

She rubs her hands together, scattering dust motes. She steps in. They must make way. This is easier than the funeral, all the eyes on her. Walking down the aisle, she imagined she still held the stale scent of the planes, felt as though she might be leaving her own little chemtrail. She'd meant to arrive sooner. The planes, delayed. The missed connection.

She drops the key in the bowl on the table in the front hall, looks down to find the brown lace-ups, work boots, and wellies. The same ones, or new versions of the same kind? Does it matter? She reaches down as though to touch a boot, hesitates an inch above, rises. She must tour the little house, take stock.

On his desk, her letters, all of them, by the looks of it, in precarious piles. His one tweed jacket hangs, limp, over the chair. It seems to put itself on her. The shoulder seams nearly reach her elbows. She returns to the hall, looks at herself in the mirror. Her hair, even after a day and a night in the air and another hour in the taxi and a funeral and another taxi, is still wild. She pushes it back, feels his hand as though he is still there, smoothing it the way he did at bedtime every night. The whole story through, he stroked her. She came to hate it: whisky and emptiness, both stale on his breath.

The shoes are on her feet before the thought has finished itself, the thick brown leather ones with the round laces and smooth soles. Her feet swim in them. She's a wee girl again, for a moment, with a daddy who is strong and sure. She stands, looks herself in the eyes. *Might as well be him.* The eyes, the aquiline nose, the broad hands, the height of her. Just her leanness and the hair give her away. She closes her eyes. More than a moment is too much. She switches to the shoes that fit. She slides the urn into one of the pockets of the jacket, so much bigger than the ones on her own.

Outside, a low grey sky. Rain. That's an exaggeration. Mist, really. As though the sky itself is drawing down, stretching thin as gauze to touch the ground. It *has* rained, though, hard, in the night. Sometimes it's what *has* happened that matters. She marches down the straight line of the thin garden path, ignoring the splash she creates with each step. *What difference does another drop make to a drowning man?* Her father, thirty years ago, hunched over the kitchen table, bills and bottle in front of him.

At the top of the hill, moor. Miles of tufty grass roll out and out into the mist. She relies on memory to tell her what's ahead. East, less than half a mile, there's the skinny road that winds inward, thirty-seven miles to the city. West, a quarter of a mile and then the land drops into the sea. South, moor and moor until the land rolls down to what's left of the village of Stratheil.

Her earliest memories are of being on his shoulders the whole way round the road and up the hill and across. She thought he was tired when he put her down just before the land began to fall, at the first sight of the edge of the village. They sat under an old oak, side by side, hand in hand. They said nothing. She didn't know they were looking for something. When he was ready, he lifted her again onto his shoulders, tromped down the hill and into the park: a shot on the swings and then ice creams on the grass. Who cared if they got green marks on their bums? He never remembered to bring a traveling rug.

When she reaches the oak, she stands close to its thick trunk, sheltering under the branches. Even naked, as they are at this time of year, they still keep the mist at bay. From her pocket, she pulls a small boule of brown bread. Boule is generous. It's really a roll, a shop-bought imitation of what her father made. It's in a plastic baggy, along with a piece of cheese. She tries to tell herself it's the same. He baked the perfect amount for three: Emilia, himself and the birds. His broad fingers mixed salt, soda, flour. *Barely mix it. You don't want it tough.* His mother's recipe, from Ireland, he said.

He marked the round with the back of a butter knife, an X on top. He thought it was for good luck, or some sort of symbol. How many years later did Emilia find out it was really to control where the crust broke? No surprise that he hadn't known that.

Under the oak, Emilia sinks to a squat, bum a few centimeters off the ground. She uses her knees as a table, breaks the bun in half, inserts one piece of cheese. She sets it on the baggy. Into the pocket again she submerges her hand, this time coming up with a flask, same as they had on those childhood walks. That's a lie. Daddy gave Emilia a flask with a cup on top, filled with steaming, strong, milky tea. Just a touch of sugar. Now, she runs a thumb across the tarnished silver of her father's flask, never polished. She sips the malt. Dailuaine. An old, obscure favorite. "Just like me," he'd said. Strong and complex, not recognized or given credit like the bigger names. Left behind.

A mouthful of bread, a sip of whisky. Irish bread. Scotch whisky. Australian woman (can she say that now?). She stops halfway through the roll and cheese, breaks off a wee bit of the bread, crumbles it at the base of the tree.

The cap back on the flask, the sandwich back in its plastic, she rises, tucks them into one pocket; she pats the other. She lets the sleeves dangle below her hands. He was a big man, her dad—long-limbed and broad as well. The kind of body that could serve as shelter or crush anything in its way. And a mind to match. As she walks away from the tree, she feels suddenly weary, as though she has never stopped walking since the morning she packed her rucksack at eighteen.

"Just the summer," she'd written. She propped the note on his desk, closed the door quietly, even though he wasn't there. She'd meant to come back at the end of the summer, hadn't she? Or is that exaggeration? Everything seems distorted now.

The rain increases. *Welcome home.* A gull, wild overhead, swoops as though he knows she still has bread. She stops and shelters her eyes from the drops.

When she'd hung up after the neighbor phoned to tell her, she'd been struck by the taste of the bread in her mouth, as though she'd freshly eaten some. She thought to bake, went to the cabinet, searched for the ingredients, sighed. What? How much? Should she Google it? Would she remember if she just got started? She went, instead, to the Irish pub three streets over. She told the barman, garnered a second round on the house. And then a third.

She kept playing back their last phone call.

"You could come home. You know, have a wee visit." His voice slow and slurred.

"This is home, now, Dad." She'd been in her flat for nearly a year—the longest yet, had even taken to feeding a half-feral cat. She swirled her drink.

"Aye."

"Do you need something?"

"What is it you think I cannae dae on my own?"

Put down the bottle. Walk a new path. Live.

She'd been seven before she realized it wasn't normal to live in a cottage with just your dad. All the days in the park with ice cream, all to the walks to get there, two years in school and into the third. And then she'd invited Roxi Dakers home. They lay on the floor of the front room, sun streaming through the bay window, coloring. Dad wheeled in the three-level tray with biscuits and milk. When he left the room, Roxi leaned over to Emilia.

"Where's your mum?" she whispered.

"I haven't got a mum," Emilia replied. She dunked her biscuit in her milk.

"Everyone has a mum."

Heat in her face. The biscuit dripping milk onto her paper below. A thud, low in the belly, which she would later learn to name as shame.

"No they haven't." She tried to sound sure.

"They have to. Everybody comes from their mum. My mum says so."

Her dad in the doorway.

"When you girls finish your biscuits, we'll walk Roxi home."

She wasn't surprised when they turned for the hill after Roxi stepped inside her house, her mother saying thank you and we'll have to have Emilia round and nice of you to walk her home. She wasn't surprised when they sat under the oak.

"I should have told you. You have a mum. She just isn't here." His big shoulders heaved a huge sigh. "C'mon up here." He lifted her up in one swoop. "Tell me the view as we walk, and I'll tell you about your mum."

A tinker. A Traveller. They used to come round every spring. Park their caravans in the meadow at the edge of town. The same place the fun fair set up in late summer. A different kind of traveler, then. When he was a boy, they used to sit on the hill and watch them, fascinated, the children seeming happy and free. He'd met the girl first when they were twelve. He'd seen her every spring after that.

She stayed with him a year after she fell pregnant. They married.

"She tried. It wasn't in her nature to be still. And it wasn't in mine to move. I thought she'd be back the next spring. I'm sorry." He hung his head. He squeezed her hand. "We're still married."

How had the truth remained painless until it was named?

Emilia began to imagine her mother a banished princess. She imagined her an adventuress, roaming the world. At thirteen, she thought she might look for her. The address on the birth certificate was her own. She did a project at school about all of Scotland's Travellers. And then one about European ones. She Googled the name. She tried not to wonder what she would say if she found her. By the time she was fifteen, she wished he'd just said she was dead.

Had his drinking increased after that day on the hill when he told her, or did she just begin to notice it then?

When she first left, she thought she could walk away, start herself freshly. Wherever she went, someone asked if she missed her mother. She tried to step into other people's imagination of her and her waiting family: Mum, Dad, a wee Scottie dog with a tartan collar. The longer she stayed away, the easier it was to believe it.

Sorry, Dad.

On the moor, she begins to trot. *Sorrysorrysorry.* She jogs into the village. She buys two ice creams and carries them to the park. She bins them both, then sticks her hand into the pocket that holds the small urn. She intended to toss him here—let the wind carry him. She hesitates. *It wasn't in my nature to move.* She pockets him again, moves on.

In the doorway to the McCaslan, his pub, she stands, hair plastered to her head.

"What'll it be?" The barman has his back to her. He turns. He scans the jacket, nods. He puts the dram on the counter. Dailuaine. "Am I right?"

She turns the glass. She nods.

A clock ticks. Some country song twangs from the radio.

"We went to school thegethir."

She sips. He turns back to what he was doing when she entered. "He loved her. I mind her pacing the moor, great round belly. She tried. So did he. People can only hold in their nature for so long."

"Across the moor?"

"Aye. Same path your father took to get here, when he could have come round the road far faster. Same path he took you."

She'd walked her mother's footsteps from the beginning.

She tilts the rest of the dram back.

"Emilia?"

"Aye." The word, held in for years, yet still so at home in her mouth.

"He missed you."

The thud, low in the belly.

The barman, Michael—she remembers now—turns to her. "He understood."

She tips back the glass, settles it gently, empty, on the bar.

She stands, dripping, at the door, can't resist the impulse to speak. She means to say she's there. *Hallo. Hiya.* "I'm home," she calls. The truth breaking out. She hangs his coat on the chair, removes her shoes, slides into his. She clomps to the kitchen, opens the recipe drawer. They are all still there, in the square block of his printing. She lifts one frail page and then another, searching. And then she comes to a page with a swirl of script: *Emilia's Traveller Bread.* Her eyes blur as she reads. This is the bread he made all those years. Not Irish bread at all. Not *his* mother's recipe.

She closes the drawer. She curls her toes inside her father's shoes. She doesn't need a recipe. She lines the ingredients up on the counter, just enough for three. She pulls the urn from her pocket. Into the bowl, she pours flour, salt, soda, milk, ashes, ashes, ashes. She closes her eyes, feels her hands in the dough, her mother's recipe, her father's ashes, the closest they have ever been.

Sacrament of Reconciliation

Ciaràn Dempsey fixed cars. Specifically, he fixed my mum's BMW. Often. The repairs were obviously exhilarating and exhausting. I deciphered this from the way Mum sat, flushed, on the burgundy velour sofa when I came home from my school, which was also a convent, on repair days.

Mum's body curved back into the low-slung middle chair of the sectional. It was the same one we'd had before we moved to Ireland, only then it had been creamy leather. My cat had clawed it relentlessly, so it got recovered for its new life. So, apparently, had my mum.

"Ciaràn," she'd breathe, as though he was still there. "Fixed it."

Most days, I came in through the kitchen and tried to glide, unnoticed, down the small hall that led to my room. On Ciaràn days, Mum seemed always able to catch me.

"We went for a test drive. Got up to 90 miles an hour." She'd sip her scotch. "It's definitely working now."

But a week or so later, some wee noise would start. "Germans," she'd mutter. She'd follow with something about the war, something about how you couldn't trust them. Ciaràn was different: young, Irish, trustworthy. Not a warrior, not at all.

In school, Sister Mary Francis had been preparing me for confession. I was behind, owing to the fact that my Scottish family wasn't Catholic. In her cramped office behind our classroom, Sister Mary Francis taught me about sins, the venial and the mortal. I'd begun to think about what to confess; I feared I may have committed more than venial sins. Hadn't I envied Siobhan her new shoes, the ones with little heels? Snuck extra bites of mashed potatoes at Easter dinner? Been proud of my ability to keep my best friend's secrets? I had committed nearly half of the mortal sins. What would happen if I confessed? And what of my mother, if she couldn't confess her own mortal sin? As I prepared, I imagined Mum's confession.

Bless me Father, for I have sinned. And then the list:

I have let Ciaràn Dempsey repair my car. A lot.

I have let him drive my car, fast, down curvy roads and across bumpy bumpy terrain and over hills, peaks, into valleys and nooks and crannies.

Ciaràn has tested the brakes in some of those nooks and crannies. He has idled there. He has revved the engine and then zoom, zoom, zoomed down that straight bit of road between the village and the city of Cork, along the River Bandon.

Bless me Father, for Ciaràn and I have braked and idled and zoomed all over County Cork, once even stopping at the shrine of Our Lady between Kinsale and Summer Cove.

I imagined myself kneeling in the confessional, holding my lips close to the grate, whispering the words on her behalf—a venial sin, perhaps, but worth it if I could say a few extra Hail Marys and absolve us both.

Celestial Navigation

OPHIUCHUS

A cloudless night, the waters calm, stars clear: she will load the skiff. The sea, flat at first, will whip when the sun begins to make herself known. By then, Isobel will be on open water.

"No place for a girl," her father said decades ago.

She'd stood on the shore, watched him go. This time, toes in the water, she will look up: Ophiuchus lowering, the night preparing to depart. She will mark the brightest of its stars. Alpha Ophiuchi, Rasalhague, from the Arabic, Head of the Serpent Collector. Her father taught her how to measure from them, so that she would know where she was in the world. When she was small, he pointed them to her from the shore, then from his own boat. Later, he made her navigate, but never on her own. Before the stars, her mother had whispered the legends of the land to her—the ancient tales of the Morrigan, Queen Scáthach of Skye, of fairies and queens, warriors and goddesses. After her father pointed out the constellations, though, she cared only for the truths of the skies.

Looking skyward, she will remember her father's whisper: Ophiuchus, the serpent bearer, connected to the Asclepius, the physician who learned from the snake how to heal so well as to bring the dead back to life.

Of course, she doesn't know what she'll do on that cloudless night a year away yet; she's still trying to shed the past as she climbs into the one-way hire car. Barely out of the car park at Glasgow Airport, she rolls down her own window, presses her glasses tightly to her face, lets her long, graying hair curl around the outside of the car. She tries to avoid thinking of her children; she tries not to feel she is running away from home.

Not so very long ago, she'd thought this would be the sort of thing she'd do with her husband. The children were nearly grown, then. She had begun imagining the house empty; she and her husband would become adventurers again.

It's been three years since he ended their twenty-five-year marriage. Four children, a house, two dogs, a cat, a scatter of bicycles, kayaks, all split in half, one way or another. He handed her a note and walked out the door.

In the car, she sighs. Isn't this an adventure? So she'd been half right. She looks down at her hand. Three years and the mark of his ring is still there. I've done right by the children, haven't I?

As she rides along, one of her children is doing a summer study in Greece. Another, a university drop-out, roams the California coast. One hunches over a desk, taking summer school to graduate early, as Isobel would have done at that age. The eldest is racking up debt, doing her second post-grad. She'd be sitting on her own somewhere. She might as well go where she wants. Mightn't she?

She has sold her house, set off for the other side of the world, near where she began. Just for the summer, she said, when she started looking for holiday lets. Then she found herself, pen poised over the lease agreement, asking for longer. She got a year, fifty-two constellations, likely including over a thousand millimeters of rain and 128 kph winds.

Isobel thinks of the wind and rain as she hurtles round the curves toward the Kyles of Lochalsh. Over the hump of the bridge, onto this largest island of the chain and the closest to mainland Scotland, her heart and stomach churning, she drops the car at the designated spot, fifteen miles from her destination. In her younger years, with a decent pair of trainers, she'd have run it in a couple of hours, slugged down a dark pint at the end. She can still cope with the pint.

Backpack snuggled against her body, she turns down the sheeptrack; she high-steps across the moor for the last of it.

Outside the cottage, later, at waters' edge, she bends her body, folds forward, closes her eyes. The clippers buzz. Hair falls to the pebbles. Silver strands lift to the wind, float out on the waters. The wind nuzzles her head. Above her, the moon rises. On the sea below it, a skiff.

SCORPIUS

Sink the shovel into black soil, heave up a huge clod, turn it; repeat. There is no full-service supermarket on the island. A garden's the trick—root vegetables and lettuce. Never mind that this should have been done in the spring, she'll try, here under summer skies. There's only herself, and she a wee thing again after all these years, the robust times of pregnancy and the clinging weight after now gone. She stands, smooths her skirt over her hips.

Did she really hate the extra pounds or was it more the look in Andrew's eye she wanted to shed? He didn't mind the extra bra size that came with it. She rests on the shovel; recalls her struggles with those last ten pounds. She laughs at her younger self.

The skiff catches her eye again: wooden, likely handmade. Clinker built. She can tell, even from this distance.

She takes to watching it from the kitchen window.

On the third morning, under a full moon, a man makes for it, hair like a sheep's, unshorn for too long, beard similar, limbs like an Irish wolfhound, gangly and looking as though they might act on an impulse of their own at any minute.

He is in the water, waders sloshing, by the time she reaches the pebbled beach. Scorpius in the sky; her father's voice in her head: the little scorpion, sent by Artemis and Leto to battle Orion. The little scorpion, beating the mighty hunter, ascending to heaven.

Here, so far north, the end of the scorpion's tail and stinger rest out of sight, below the horizon. Isobel turns landward, spots the croft, white in the moonlight, hunkered further back than her cottage, as though it is hiding. If he came from there, he would be her next-door neighbor. Her only neighbor.

In her former neighborhood, in the suburbs of Atlanta, with its winding cul-de-sacs meant to look like quaint country roads, the neighborly thing would have been for his wife to come over with a pan of brownies or a plate of chocolate chip cookies. Perhaps his wife doesn't bake. Perhaps it isn't the custom here. Perhaps he hasn't got a wife.

The pebbles press against the soft soles of her feet. What must she look like, there on the shore, stubbly head, skinny white legs sticking out under her skirt? She folds her arms.

He climbs into the boat, lifts oars, looks up when he is seated, settled, ready to take the first pull. She waves. The oars hover above the water. A gull calls. The oars move back, sink in. His body leans back. Pull. Her father, in the pond at Mull, on holiday. "Pull, girl. Have you any muscles in those arms at all?" She rubs her bicep, makes for the cottage. When the sun is fully up, she returns with a blanket, book, knitting, a flask of tea.

By the time he rounds the corner into the bay, the wind has picked up, the sun gone behind the clouds. Still, she shelters under her wide-brimmed hat. Likely, she doesn't need it with her at all, here near the top of the world, come as she has from so much closer to the equator. There, finely grained sand burned her feet at the height of summer. Searing rays reached into skin, feeling as though the veins, even, burned.

When her children were small, they spent weekends at the coast. She scrimped to hide small change from what her husband allocated for groceries; secreted the children away to the sea while he went for boys' weekends in the mountains. She wanted them to know the expanse of water. One on her hip, three behind, ducklings with shade hats flapping as they ran behind her, skin coated in SPF 95. She felt as though she was wrapped in cling film, suffocating.

Now, in the little bay, pebbles under the blanket dig into her bum. She smiles, sits straighter, knits another row. Her book lies face down, spine broken. The tea is long finished.

He wades in, a herd of fish on a huge hook, held tight. She's reminded of a boy she loved in college: a fly fisher, tickly bearded, on the fast-track to drop-out, standing at her door, a shining trout, with staring eyes, in each hand.

"Can I take you to dinner?" the boy asked. He drove them to a campsite on a trail just north of town. He tossed foil-wrapped potatoes into a fire he'd already built, dressed the fish. They ate with their hands. Two weeks before the end of the semester, he stuffed his decrepit Mazda full, except for the passenger seat.

"Come with me."

She shook her head, went back to her books. Another year before Summa Cum Laude and a ring on her left hand.

When Charlotte, her eldest, was three, the same boy arrived at her door, a trout in each hand, again.

"I'm married," she said.

"I heard. Does it kill your taste buds?" He held them out. "I wanted to make sure you're happy."

She nodded, ignoring the clench in the gut. He kissed her cheek. "Hope he likes them." His dreadlocks bounced as he made his way to the car.

She buried the fish in the freezer.

Her husband found them months later.

"Why do we have trout?"

"They were a good deal," she said. She felt a flush begin, cleared her throat.

"You know I hate trout."

She took them to the beach, built a fire, tossed in potatoes, ears of corn. She ate one whole herself, fed her daughter small bites of the other.

Now, she squints at the huddle of fish. She's forgotten all that swims in these waters. Perhaps she should have done some more research before she packed up her house, stepped onto the plane. Too late now. She smiles.

The man hesitates on the shore, looks up the hill, then glances toward her. He turns in her direction. Slowly, she rises. Her hand floats up as though to take off her hat. She remembers her shorn head, lowers the hand, extending it when he is within reach.

"You're not from here," he says, glancing at her bronzed skin.

"I started here," she says. "Near enough. Just been away for a wee while." As though she's been on holiday. For thirty years.

"Aye," he says. His eyes measure from under eyebrows like caterpillars, the hairy kind the children were afraid to touch in the back garden.

"Nice catch," she says.

"No bad," he says. "You must be the new tenant. For the summer?"

"For the year," she says.

"That so?"

"Aye," she says, feeling the sound of her childhood in her mouth.

"A whole turn?" One of the caterpillars arches.

"Longest I could get."

"That so?"

"Mm."

He extends his hand. His fingers, rough and damp, wrap round her still-smooth ones.

"Archie," he says.

"Isobel."

"I'll see you again, I'm sure, between now and the end. Particularly if you sit on the shore all the morning." He turns, the fish still over his shoulder. Ten shining eyes stare at her as he moves away, feet lifting a little too high with each step over the stones, fish patting him on the back as he goes.

She removes her hat; she is rubbing her stubbly head when he glances back.

Long ago, her father hunched over a hull, one grey winter day. Sawdust in his dark hair made him look older than his time. At four years old, she approached the boat, his first. He looked up, hands still on the hull, his dark eyes meeting hers. She reached for the smooth wood, closed her eyes. She sniffed, and then leaned forward, tongue out, tasted. He laughed. She opened her eyes, found him beside her. He lifted her, then, and carried her inside.

"I'll let you help on the next one," he said, setting her down by her mother.

His friend Michael came, when it was ready. She followed as they carried it to the shore, small toes gripping the pebbles. The men pushed the boat, waded in after it. The sea lapped at her feet, cold. The men climbed in. She thought her father might come for her; she thought of wading in after them, farther than she was allowed. She stood still, whispering his instruction, no higher than your knees. She had never disobeyed. The dress her mother had knitted for her clung to her pale legs. Her father lifted one oar, then the other. He pulled.

She stepped out of the waters when he rounded the corner out of sight. She made her way to the workshop, damp feet gathering sawdust as she padded. By the time she entered the kitchen, her feet looked like two small fish, battered and ready to be cooked.

They lived at a lower latitude then, farmlands and hills like gentle green waves rolling away from the sea, the scents of seaweed and shit mingled. In childhood, she fought the urge to wrinkle her nose or pinch it closed. She might have given in to it except she hated the squawking of the ringleted girls in her class who did those sorts of things. Later, it became one of her comfort smells, reminding her of the solidity of land as well as the wideness of the sea, the latter her preference. Nourishment for body and soul.

As she grew, she began to want to test the waters, alone. "That's no place for a girl," he repeated. He used the voice reserved for immutable decisions.

She reminded herself that he allowed her everything else: the making of bait, the careful attachment to the hooks, the casting, the reeling in. He'd leap, though, if she seemed to struggle. From the shore, on her own, she'd hauled in a couple of large fish, bigger than her father's usual. She'd gasped at the sight of them there on the hook, pulled them close, sunk fingers into them, held firmly as she pulled back the hook.

Side by side, they scraped the scales, gutting the insides, blood running, heads in a pile, removed because her mother feared the eyes. She stood beside him at the grill, helping if there was a large batch on. But he'd never, ever given her control of the boat.

"A tide could catch you. A rogue wave. A wake from one of those arsehole speedboats, a storm. And look at you, a lovely wee thing. How would you ever fight it?" He'd kissed her head. "I would never forgive myself."

PISCES

Her father's work moved them three thousand miles, across the ocean, to a town hundreds of miles from the coast, craggy hills rising, mountain streams burbling down. He put his boats in dry-dock—they'd be back in a year, two at the most.

Isobel took to the rivers, learned the flies, bought her own waders with money earned from her job at the mall. At first, the rivers felt small, constrained. Land, rising steeply on either side; another voice, limiting where she could go. It was the only water offered, though. Joy took her by surprise, growing in her with each step as she learned to read the river. These close waters offering multiple paths. When she discovered trout huddled under rocks, she felt as though she'd been made privy to a long-held secret. She loved being out, alone, deciding how long to rest in one place, when to move.

Her father hated river fishing. She'd heard him groan about going up the Spey with friends. Still, she talked him into joining her once, a hot day too early in the season. He thrashed in the water, not used to being the vessel itself, unable to glide as she did.

It wasn't until he died, fifteen years after they moved, of a sudden heart attack, that she discovered that he'd sold the boats to pay for her college. A second death: no chance, then, to run her hand across the wood her father had worked, to hold him again in this way.

On the island, a windy day in September, skirts billowing, she passes an angler on a rocky promontory. He casts, waits, casts again. She notices the familiar tightening of the back muscles. Her own back tenses. She walks on. Sheep graze among the hummocks of grass.

She finds an out-of-the-way edge of shore for the first go. Only one tiny fish is tempted. Back it goes. The next day, one worth keeping. She braves the more popular spots, nets a few one day. They bounce over her shoulder on the way home, as if to say, "Well done, you!"

No matter which direction she comes from, she finds herself compelled to stop at the center of the bay before turning up the path to the cottage, to face the boat. She imagines the feel of the hull, the oars within to pull her to the open sea.

She casts from the shore before dawn, not there in the bay but at the edge of a promontory nearly a mile from the croft. She pauses at the second decent-sized sea trout, looks skyward, finds Pisces.

Two fish, tails tied together, who helped Aphrodite and her son Eros escape the monster, Typhus.

She casts again, catches a third. Plenty. One for supper, two to freeze. Both fridge and freezer are tiny, barely the space for the ice trays, which she has removed to make room. She never picked up the habit of ice anyway.

Rod in one hand, bucket in the other, fish gathered on one hook, she steps back. A mist settles. The particles expand, become drizzle. Moments later, they turn to engorged drops of rain. Soaked, at the edge of the water, she tilts her head, sticks out her tongue, becomes self-conscious, pulls it back in. Might he be watching?

In the cottage, she puts the cleaned fish in the fridge and freezer. Goosebumps rise all over; she draws a bath. In it, she has to bend, knees high, scrunch to submerge her head, stubble now starting to regrow in the direction of something like hair, though it will be a long time before it is long enough to float out around her as it used to. She imagines herself a trout in the waters, free. Her younger self hadn't known the difference between nourishment and false lure; she'd bitten at the bait: the cut of the hook in her lip, the haul into useless air, gills flapping, struggle futile, collapsing in on herself. If she'd been deemed too small, been lucky enough to be thrown back in, would she have been wise enough to resist a second time?

ERIDANUS

In the dark before an unseasonably warm March dawn, she sheds her sheer skirt, leaves it in a jumble with her boots and socks on the pebbled shore as though they've been removed by a lover, too carried away by the moment to place them neatly. She slides herself into the wetsuit that Charlotte insisted she bring—her skin, having returned to its original pale, seems almost luminous in the moonlight. She wades out to the boat. She tells herself she does not care if he catches her. She can swim away.

Rain begins. Fat drops land on her head, arms, shoulders, softly and each with enough volume to make it seem as though they might bounce before bursting. The rain comes harder and faster. At the edge of the boat, she holds out her arms, open to the sky and sea; she closes her eyes. Cool waters dot her eyelids, the tip of her nose, her lips. She opens her mouth, catches drops on the tongue, swallows. She reaches out until she feels the solidity of the hull. Varnished wood, smooth and wet, down the side, all the way from one end of a strake to the other. She stretches her palm below the surface of the water, runs her fingers down across each ridge of overlapping plank.

Isobel lifts her hand from the water, runs it over her shaggy hair. Taking in a deep breath, she opens her eyes but does not glance at the shore. In she goes, sitting in the belly for only a moment before stretching herself flat. The rain slows, then stops, the air still humid, wrapping around her. She drifts within herself.

A wave rocks her. She opens her eyes but resists the impulse to sit up, check that the boat is tethered. Hasn't she watched it rest here for days on end, safe? In the sky, Eridanus. Phaeton taking over his father's chariot, unable to control it, scorching earth and heaven. Zeus striking him dead and casting him to earth.

Her arms tense, biceps aching, a haunting sensation that accompanies the memory of tiptoeing out of the house on one of the rare nights her father went on another man's boat.

They had been out together that afternoon, she and her father, the skies and waters smooth, like blue ice and them in a sliver of warmth above. They'd nearly been lulled to sleep waiting for a bite, bundled as they were in winter gear and that day, too, unseasonably warm. Not a word said in the reeling and gutting. He let her row home. The oars slid into the water with the merest tinkle, gliding through. A few clouds gathered outside the kitchen window as she stood beside her mother, peeling potatoes. The air remained still.

Her father scraped back his chair after dinner, rubbed his tummy, a paunch beginning above the belt, balanced by long legs and broad shoulders.

"Lovely. Thank you, ladies," he said. He tucked his chair under. "That's me away to Billy's, then. We're out early. Away up the Spey." He shook his head. "I'll never understand the call of closed water. However."

In the wee hours, Isobel lay awake, thinking of the boat, left near water's edge for her father's convenience. Sometimes after these river trips, he took to the sea before he even came into the house.

A Friday night. Her mother would have her one long lie of the week; Dad not being there, Mum would make it a good one.

Perhaps the slight whip of wind just outside the front door should have been warning enough. Or the stumble on the pebbles, knee scraped, warm blood running. She wiped the stream with her index finger, licked it clean, pushed the boat, jumped in, looked skyward, read in it the preamble to dawn. Isobel settled her hands comfortably on the oars, pulled, too happy to note that her progress might have been a little too easy.

Her father had taught her well how to read the skies. She could navigate her way around the whole of the northern hemisphere if need be.

He'd never taught her how to read the water. Why would it have occurred to her that he'd let her pull only when the waters were with her?

When she rounded the corner out of the bay, she faced the hump of rising sun; she took a few more strokes. She hadn't brought pole or bait. It was her intent to be back before anyone knew she'd been gone. A fish would only have been evidence against her.

She pulled in the oars, leaned back, closed her eyes, and rested. When she opened them, a scant five minutes later, the landscape had changed. She spun around in her seat to be sure what she was seeing was right. The hump of Banford Head, below which she'd closed her eyes, was now well behind her, the curve into the bay far back indeed. She brushed hair from her face, stuck in the oars, pulled herself breathless, paused, turned. Had she made any gain at all? She turned forward again, hair blinding her. In the pause while she tucked her hair into her jacket, the boat lost its small gain. Her arms ached. She gauged the sun. Hours before her mother would waken. And then why would she think Isobel would go for the boat? Another day before her father would come for it.

If she let herself drift with the tide, how far would it carry her before it turned? She continued to pull, afraid to trust the water, afraid to trust herself.

The trawler found her red-faced, tear-stained, blisters having formed and burst. Her arms and back burned within her slicker and jumper and skin. She pointed homeward, words seeming impossible. They weren't necessary. The fishermen knew the boat. One of them climbed down and in with her.

"Your dad'll have warned you about this?"

She nodded, eyes cast down.

"You've to read the waters, girl. Make them do the work for you."

He rowed her to the wide entry to the bay, climbed back up to his trawler.

The wind had stilled. The tide had begun to turn.

"You'll be alright now."

The larger vessel idled as she rowed. She felt the eyes on her as she pulled to shore, dragged the boat up, wiped her blood from the oars.

In the house, the clink of her mother's coffee cup landing in the kitchen sink greeted her.

"Hi Mum. Just going for a bath to warm up," she called, taking the stairs two at a time.

The water, still and small and safe around her, held her shame and her secret. Decades later, in the skiff, she feels it all again.

Overhead a gull calls. She closes her eyes again, rocks. When she opens them, he is at the edge of the boat. He sets his gear in the boat—enough for both of them. Silent, he reaches for her hand, pulls her to sitting. He climbs in. He casts off.

When the first bite comes on her line, he leans toward her. She pays no mind, plays out the line, reels in. The pole bends and straightens; her spine moves with it. She finds it hard to root herself, bum on the seat, bare feet in the bow. His hand rises. Her lips turn upward, very slightly, as she plays out the line one last time, shifting her body just enough to block his help.

The creature, a feisty few pounds, rocks the boat when it flops in. Archie nods, turns, casts. His marker bobbing, he looks again in the bucket. He looks at her. She hesitates, one hand on the hook, the other pinching bait, as though she's twelve again, digging her hands into a bucket of worms. The only girl who would lift one out, never mind pierce the soft flesh with the hook; the only girl who sat beside Jimmy Davis and Patrick Dunn as something other than spectator. They had not so much as a nibble that day. Bored, her girlfriends went away, giggling down the path. They said she'd wasted her time. And she'd got disgusting worm guts on her hands. What boy would like her after that?

In Archie's boat now, hook in hand again, she meets his eye. Stillness in the middle of the wide sea. Bait the hook. Cast. The warmth of his back at hers, barely touching. Feel the bite. Play out the line. Reel in. Five times, then Archie turns shoreward.

On the pebbles, he faces her. "Next time, just wander over when you want to go." He slings his fish over his shoulder. "You might not have to wait so long." He ambles away, limbs once again looking as though they might set out on a journey of their own.

Dusk: over a small fire by the shore, fish sizzles. Her buttery fingers pick it apart. Licking clean the last finger, she thinks she senses him behind her. Toss the bones to the fire, pull the shawl tight, face the flames.

VIRGO

Dawn, with a sky of orange and pink. Shepherd's warning, her grandmother said. The drover's daughter. Sailor's warning, her father said, scrubbing a hull. Son of a North Sea cod fisher. She trudges to the croft anyway, sodden earth squelching. Light sneaks out under a sliver of gap at the bottom of the door. The buzz of the saw rides out after it. In the breeze, she stands, hand raised to knock. The saw stops. The air stills. The sky opens. As her hand meets the door, she feels his tug on the other side, moves with it.

Sawdust, varnish, metal, sweat—the familiar scents. She wants to sit, cross-legged, bum in sawdust, breathe. She wants to lie naked in it, rub the shaven particles across her body, make herself a seaworthy vessel. Tiny wood flakes settle in the light between them.

"Can I touch her?" she asks.

"Aye."

Hand on raw wood. He tells her he is a builder, was a hobbyist until his wife died. She feared the water. This is why they chose a croft so far from the shore.

"Imagine," he says. "Growing up on an island and being afraid of the water. She squeezed shut her eyes on the ferry to the mainland for our honeymoon, huddled in the hull on the return. Never went to the water again."

When he was four, he built his first boat, a miniature, of course. He sailed his teddy away in the bay. "They became engulfed in the first tiny wave. I cried, on the shore, sloshed in to try to help."

"Your teddy," she says.

"My boat."

Outside, the redness in sky has dissipated.

Two mornings later, she steps down to the shore, casts in one pebble. The world is silent, except for the whisper of the sea. She turns and tiptoes to his door, hesitates there, her hand aloft.

"Come," he says.

From the corner, she watches. Without asking, she lifts the broom, begins to sweep, the shavings revealing the grey stone floor.

When he has finished, he steps outside. "Not a day for it," he says.

Replacing the broom in the corner, she sets out for home, gathers her gear, drops a line at the first spot. Fresh fish for brunch.

She bakes a round of wheaten bread, her grandmother's recipe; the nutty scent of the grain trails behind her in the still afternoon air. She leaves it on the doorstep, knocks, firmly, walks away, does not look back.

When she goes again, he hands her varnish to hold.

"My father let me do this," she says. "When I was wee."

His eyes shift. He works on, fifteen minutes, half an hour, an hour, more. The scent of his sweat rises. She breathes him in.

"What else did he show you?" he asks, at last.

She tells him, in chronological order, with ages. At four, the sweeping. Five, holding the varnish.

"At ten, he caught me stroking the lathe. He sent me to my room. Shouted about the danger. He woke me a week later, though, at three in the morning. Took me down. Held my hand in his as we guided the wood through."

As she finishes the list, the wind picks up outside, rattles the windows as though it wants in. He waits to speak until the sky has finished her turn.

"Everything?"

"Everything." Except the sea. She helped him build, and then watched her father and the boat float off. A little like children. Or husbands. The closest she'd come was when she had been a vessel herself—swollen, round, sinking into water at the last, midwife at her side, her husband in the corner.

Seven pounds, nine ounces, the first, a lassie. She'd been afraid, at first, that she might not know what to do with a girl.

Nine pounds, two ounces, the second, a boy (what her father wanted).

Over ten, the next. Same again.

And then the last, arriving early, four flopping pounds. Another lassie.

Isobel holds all this to herself there in his workshop, the wind rattling again, her face flushed in the cold.

He steps close. Lips on her forehead. His white hair electrified as his hands cup her cheeks. Her hands hang loosely at her sides, oars at the ready.

She works beside him for the rest of the boat. When the client pulls up, a fat man in a Range Rover, from the mainland, the south, she imagines him rowing the boat out to his yacht. Archie and Isobel hold hands, watch the vessel go.

She orders wood, varnish, the lot, online. As she gathers her supplies, she does not allow herself to imagine what she will do if he says no. She carries all of it, piece by piece, to his croft. When the last of it is there, she knocks, even though they are beyond that, now.

When he opens the door, the skies are clear. Heather climbs the hillsides, purple bells in full bloom. He stands, feet planted, legs wide, hands on hips. His tufty hair lifts in a drift of breeze. She waits for him to look up, holds his eyes when he does.

"I want to build it on my own."

"Course you do," he says.

She thinks she sees a slight clench. In the moment, she attributes it to his thinking about the loss of his space and the use of his tools for the time it will take her.

He checks on her as she goes.

When it is finished, he helps her carry it to the water. She pushes it out, leaves it at anchor beside his.

OPHIUCHUS

When she wades into the waters that night, she recalls his eyes on her through the long months of building, guiding her without touching, allowing her to make it perfect.

A breath in as she makes her way to her creation. Above her, a cloudless sky. Her skiff faces the shore, her cottage, Archie's croft, the mottled pebble bay, tufty grass, rising hills. If his long limbs or any other part of him have had an impulse to journey out and check on her, he has resisted: a gift of understanding.

She hears her father's whisper. No place for a girl.

Her body replies. Mark the moon, Polaris, the horizon. Climb in. Let the boat settle, haul in the anchor. Sink the oars into the waters. Pull. Out and out, around the curve of the bay. Herself and the wood and the waters, under the moon and the stars, on the wide sea.

Presently, the Tension Drains

Ina's pink-slippered feet press against the grey tile of the laundry room floor. Her sweet-pink painted nails curl around the handle of the iron. She bears down, creasing Humphrey's grey slacks.

The size of the waist of him, she thinks. *A hippopotamus would be embarrassed. And him out on that old bicycle of his. In the rain.*

The cycling might make a difference if he wasn't likely to stop off and have a latte and a cream bun at Nardini's on the front, staring out at the Firth of Clyde and the western Scottish islands beyond. Or a cup of tea and a bacon butty when he gets home, staring into the telly. Or both.

Ina turns over the trousers, lining up the edges again, pressing hard as she moves the iron over the starched polyester blend. Razors, she's after, thin blades reaching from pleated waist to cuffed ankles; razors to match what she feels, the words she wishes she could say to the adult son upstairs. Their Great Hope, he was, now turned into a great lummox, making and unmaking the same remote-controlled car day after day.

Once, the lad was champion of the physics team at university. Once, he was married to his lab partner, a brilliant girl, and with a nice, dimpled chin as well. Nearly made you not notice the buckteeth. Cecil hadn't noticed, anyway, until a few months ago.

"I've just gone off her, Mum," he said, dragging his suitcase up the front stairs to his old room just the other day.

He's gone off alright, Ina thinks.

She adds starch, turns the trousers again, hears the rain, harder, on the roof.

Humphrey comes dripping in just as she's lifting his double-starched, sharp-edged slacks from the ironing board. Soaked, he is, soaked through, yet somehow telltale pale dots of creamy dough still cling at the corners of his mouth. He peels off jacket, jumper, trousers; he keeps going—vest, socks, underpants.

Humphrey stands, wrinkly pink toes on the smooth tile.

"Shove over, darlin'." He elbows her, lightly. "I've to dry my skivs here."

There's something else that's gone off, Ina thinks.

The white Y-fronts flop onto the ironing board, wet. Ina has a pile of laundry and anger to work through. And now there'll be a wet spot on the ironing board.

Humphrey's pale legs seem to sprout directly from his tummy. He reminds Ina a wee bit of a Mr. Potatohead from her childhood. They used actual potatoes when she was a girl—poked stray buttons and other bits in for their eyes and nose and so on. Twigs from the garden for legs, modeling clay feet.

Humphrey's whale hump of a belly jiggles slightly as he runs the iron over the cotton, drying one side with the heat. He flips the underpants to the other side, not moving them to a dry spot. His tongue reaches for the edge of his mouth, perhaps in concentration. It finds and curls around the cream puff remnant.

Ina slides out of her slippers, turns for the door, pulls on her wellington boots. She steps out.

"Only be another minute," Humphrey calls after her.

Ina marches, she doesn't know where, in the direction of the sea, the frothy Firth of Clyde like an ocean of freshly pulled pints. Not normally a drinker at all, Ina thinks she might fancy one today. She passes the pub, though, but stops short of the sea, diverting herself with the park at the end of the close.

Snowdrops huddle at the feet of the trees. Ina leaves the path, sloshes across the wet grass, slumps in front of a cluster of them. She admires the slender stalks, wonders at the delicate flowers, so bold as to bloom in the face of the Scottish winter and with the good sense to keep their heads down. Shrouded in white petals, they see only their slim green stalks and never have to face cloud or wind or rain. What snow might fall is landed, settled, peaceful by the time it comes under their gaze.

Ina leans over, vaguely realizing that the wet has soaked through her jacket and trousers and underpants already. She grasps a stalk, gently at first, between thumb and forefinger. Ina squeezes. She bends the stalk backward. She pulls, snapping the wee white head right off. The rain slackens. The wind stills a bit. The wet spreads down her legs. She drops the first head, not even looking. Ina reaches for another and another.

Ina has shouted at boys for doing this very thing to the daffodils that line the main street in the village. Years ago, when Cecil was fourteen or so, she shouted at him and a friend, doing the same to her very own tulips at the end of the drive. She wonders if someone will come to the park and shout at her, a woman, older than she, not that many of those exist anymore, or are fit enough to come out in this weather. She wonders if she should shout at herself.

Ina grasps, bends, snaps, drops, again and again and again until only one blossom remains.

"There." She leans closer to it. "Now we can see you."

Ina rises presently, feeling the tension drained, not caring, even, about the grass stains that surely must mark the backs of her trousers. She dusts herself off, wiggles her toes.

They are warm and dry in her wellies.

Behind the Veil

1967

April awakened the whole country with frost, Dunnet Head to Lizard Point. No sun to give a little sparkle. A low-hanging grey held the sky close. Refusing to fully open, the day inched forward. Morning wasn't yet finished when Iceland sent a deep depression south. In the east, a spitting rain. In the west, drenched Glaswegians sloshed home. All through the night and the next day, the rain continued above Hadrian's wall. Gale-force winds swept the water horizontal in the air. England sat, settled and sunny while the ships docked at the Port of Leith, near Edinburgh, creaked and rolled. Eiders, drawn by delicious mussels, instead sought shelter near the mouth of the Water of Leith, tucked into themselves; even these heaviest and fastest of the country's ducks were no match for the weather.

On the edge of my wee island, west of Glasgow and then further west, across the waters, I stood out in it, watching the mainland as though that would somehow connect me to Mary, herself tucked into a mothering home near the docks where the eiders sheltered, on the opposite side of the country. They said this was best, the only way—to send her away, to keep the secret at all costs. Mary would rest, be among others like her, return to build a new life, unmarked.

Later, she would tell me that they made the girls knit. They sat, side by side, yarn around fingers and knitting pins: through, around, over, out, again and again to make the layette for a child they would never be allowed to see, much less hold. The thrash of the winds outside. Rivulets running down the glass, conjoining and separating again and again. The sobbing of the girls, of the knitted stitches becoming one little arm and then another, the matron's staccato, "This is right. This is right. This is right." Her cruel words bashing at Mary from the outside. The baby bashing at Mary from the inside. She felt the child knew, was angry with her already. I'd had two of my own, each different even before I saw their faces. Perhaps the baby was matching the weather, or would be an active bairn, like Mary's brother. Later, after Mary told me what happened, I imagined the child hitting back at the matron, defending the both of them.

And then, suddenly, on the thirteenth, a lazy ridge of high pressure ambled down from further north. Dry and warm and sunny, a relief. The next evening, I stepped out into the night sky to watch the aurora. In all the years I'd seen it, it felt like a blessing. That night, all I could think of was Mary and the other girls in the home. There was the faint hope that they'd been allowed to press their swollen feet into their shoes, to step outside, to receive this small blessing. Surely, they deserved a wee glimpse at the lights, the Fir Chlis, the Merry Dancers. If not that night, then the next, only that spring, the aurora was a one-night stand. And the girls were not allowed out. They missed the dance.

In the morning, the peace I normally found in the aftermath of the lights was nowhere to be found. I continued thrashing around, not so different from the bairn within Mary. I could hardly still myself all the time that Mary was gone. Hamish said I was like a bee buzzing for nectar, jumping from flower to flower. I didn't feel nearly so nice as that; inside, I felt like a cleg—a big, black horsefly. I saw a girl bitten by one when I was a girl too. Oh, the howl she let out, and the great streak of blood running down her arm. It must have been 1936. Clegs seemed like the most dangerous thing then. Yes, that's what I felt like, thirty-one years later: black and poisonous and wanting to draw blood.

To escape myself, I cleaned the windows, the skirting boards, the floors; ironed anything that could be made flat and smooth; baked bread, with yeast instead of soda specifically because it required so much more work. Hamish snuck up behind me as I took the last round out of the oven, drawn, I assumed, by the scent. I spun around, hair wild and spattered with flour—it had been a frenzied and furious baking. Perhaps he meant to take me in his arms, to soothe me. I didn't give him the chance, holding my hand up against him, the only time I've ever done so. My horsefly self reflected in his eyes. I knew he felt no better than I, only he managed to hold it in. I could see the anger smoldering, in the tightness of his muscles beneath his shirt, his clenched jaw, the furrow between his eyebrows. I feared that if we stayed in the house together just then, I would say something harmful, blame him, when I knew it wasn't his fault. His hand on my back felt like a branding stick. My heat, his heat, the heat of the kitchen, we were a furnace, baking in our own rage and fear and powerlessness.

"I'll just take some air before tea," I said. I couldn't meet his eye as I passed. I didn't brush his cheek or lips with mine, the only time I'd ever left the house without doing so. I did not sit to put on my walking shoes, barely noticed the pile of wood and rubble he'd stacked in the back, as though preparing for an uncharacteristic bonfire.

Away from the village, around the curve of the south end of the island, I marched. The water lapping at my side seemed too kind. I refused to be soothed so easily. I turned inland and up, skirting the edges of the fields of the Ross' farm. I wanted my feet on the ground and my face in the sky; those could be trusted. I held my pace across the top and down the other side, not thinking, until I arrived at the far end of the village. I realized, then, that I still wore my apron, covered in flour. I might have gone through the village like that, looking like a madwoman—it wouldn't have been the first time that there had been whispers to that effect. Worse than that would have been someone asking after Mary. Perhaps I shouldn't have cared; perhaps I should have marched right through like haughty Mrs. MacInnes. I couldn't bring myself to. Mary would be coming back. Perhaps, I dared to hope, having had a change of heart, with my first grandchild. I clung to the faint hope that there was still time to make things right. In the meantime, I didn't want anyone else's whispers falling on either of them. Like a fox, I slunk through the alleys and lanes behind the village, sniffing the air for danger along the way.

When the drift of smoke reached me, I looked to the hill. Perhaps an early Beltane fire, a celebration of fertility I might have joined in previous years. As I drew closer, I realized it was from our house. I began to run, then, fearing I'd forgotten to turn off the oven.

Out onto the street, I ran, never mind the wild hair and dirty apron. Never mind what people might say. The house came into view, solid as ever. The pile of rubble I'd dismissed came back. Hamish. What else was he planning to burn? I ran faster, hoping it wasn't what I feared, Mary's diaries. I'd seen her climb the attic stairs just a few days before I took her east, a tidy bundle under her arm. I'd recognized the edge of one of her diaries. They'd be safe there, I thought.

Hamish brought them down not long after she left, having happened upon them when he was looking for something else. "Leave them," I said. "She'll want them when she's ready." I thought he'd put them back. I didn't check. Add that to the list of things I might have done.

At the edge of the flames, a photo curled alongside the thick cover of a diary, the lock already blackening.

I bent, pulled the flaming edge of the diary from the pyre. Of course, all the pages within had already been consumed. On my haunches, there at the corner of the garden, I felt the tears begin to rise, at last, for all that I had been too weak or blind to see or do or save. I had waited for them since Mary came home in December—she and James hand in hand down the garden path. I knew before she said a word that she was pregnant.

"You've news," I whispered when she leaned in to kiss me.

"Don't be cross, Mummy." Same as when she was five and I caught her taking one of the warm pancakes from under the tea towel without asking. She knew I'd have said it would spoil her dinner.

"Of course not, pet." Not cross, scared.

"We're getting married," she said.

James beamed, looking like the cat who'd got the cream.

The door to the front room creaked behind me. James' lips straightened. His chest deflated.

"Hamish," I said, turning.

"Come in, James," Hamish said. He pulled James in fully with one hand and pushed the door shut with the other. "What've you done, son?" He held his hand on James' shoulder.

"I. We," he stammered.

"We're getting married," Mary said.

"You're scarce twenty."

"Same as I was," I said.

"You'll need to get on with it, then." He glanced at Mary, his face smooth and stoic. "They'll not let you down the aisle with." He stopped, turned to James. "What've your parents said?"

James' neck and ears reddened.

"You'll need to get on with that, then."

Mary has never told me precisely what happened at the MacInnes'. She and James went, arm-in-arm, out the front door. I went back to the kitchen to peel the potatoes. The front door slammed not half an hour later, and then there stood Mary, dry-eyed and looking as though she'd had all the air let out of her.

"Mrs. MacInnes." She sounded shocked at the sound of the name.

I waited.

"She. He. We're not getting married."

"What?"

"She won't let him."

He's an adult, I thought. She can't stop him. And then I recalled them arriving, Mrs. MacInnes glowering and running the whole show.

I pulled Mary to me. "She'll change her mind. Daddy will speak to her."

Only she wouldn't. A few days passed, and then Hamish said he'd go and speak to the lad himself.

When he went round, James was gone.

"I've sorted him," Mrs. MacInnes said, the door open only a few inches.

"Sorted?"

"He's away. Working. He can see what being an adult with no qualifications is all about."

"What about the bairn? Mary?"

"It's none of my affair what your daughter does with her baby. How do we even know who the father really is?"

I held my head high. I would not let that horrible woman shame me. Or Mary. We held it all in, for Mary's sake, and perhaps because we were afraid of what would happen if we let it out. I've never felt such rage.

For Hamish, it built up and up until he could do nothing but incinerate it all.

"Hamish?" He came from the other side of the fire to stand beside me.

"It's done. It's for the best. The way is cleared, now. She can't dwell in it. She can move on."

"We can't just pretend it didn't happen," I said. "We have to reconcile with it."

"That's what I've just done," Hamish said. "This is how I've reconciled."

Squelching the story only makes it come out in other ways. Something must rise from the ashes.

I wept, then, crouching by the fire, as though my tears could douse it. I wept for Mary. I wept for myself. Most of all, though, I wept for the bairn, who deserved, as we all do, the story of our beginnings. And Hamish had burned it.

He did not understand that you can't simply burn the bits of the story that hurt; you can't pretend. The whole tale must be told if it is to be understood. If it is denied, it will return in another form, again and again until its voice is heard. That afternoon by the fire, I felt the understanding in my whole body.

We went, Hamish and I, to visit Mary in hospital, the day after the birth. Hamish wanted his daughter, to see her safe, to get her home and begin this clean slate he thought we'd given her. I wanted more, said nothing of it as I opened the car door, stepped out, entered through the small archway with him.

Inside, down the long hall, the harsh smell of disinfectant stung my nose. It wasn't just my daughter who was there. It was her daughter, too. My grandchild. My blood. I left him to find the child, just a few steps down the hall, in the opposite direction of the ward.

There she lay, round-faced and dark-haired. Alone. The other babies taken to their mothers. Hand to glass, as close as I could get. I wanted to shatter it. To run in and claim her. It wasn't my choice, though. It was Mary's. I couldn't take that from her. She'd lost so much already. I didn't know, then, what they'd done to her in the home.

Onto the ward then. I couldn't hold it in. "Acht she's lovely. Let's just take her home." I meant it to be kind. It wasn't. Mary sat, propped on pillows, blinking, and shaking her head, that red robe James gave her for Christmas still wrapped around her. I had no idea what they'd said to her in the mothering home, that they'd convinced Mary that they had been right—Mrs. MacInnes, the matron at the mothering home, saying she wasn't fit to be a mother, not a *real mother*, saying she had done wrong, saying the only good she could do now to redeem herself, and to save the child, was to give her away, no matter what her body and her heart, never mind her mother, said. She pulled the robe tighter. It seemed that the only good I could do was to allow her this one awful choice. I've lain awake night after night wondering if that, too, was wrong. What if I had been strong enough to insist, to take charge, to claim my own kin that April afternoon?

A thick fog laid claim to us as November began. The sky refused to allow the day to fully open. When I stepped out to get the paper, I could barely make out the wall at the end of the garden. The hill behind the house hid. The road and the cove, the waters beyond, and the mainland on the other side had been taken. A fog itself is not unusual here. Perhaps it was the timing. It struck me more harshly than usual that the veil, which opens each year as Samhain approaches, had closed again. We must now stay on whichever world we awakened in, until the veil opened again. This is the way of things, yet I could say nothing of this to anyone. They would laugh, dismiss it as an old woman's nonsense. I have seen it at work, though.

As I bent to the ground, straining to hear the muffled whisper of the waves, I felt the loss final, settled, as surely as I've felt anything. I have never asked if Mary did, too. If she did, I'm sure she dismissed it. She'd gone away to Perth, to start afresh after a summer of swaying to and fro on the ferry, from this island to the Church of Scotland women on the mainland, listening to their advice, paying for the baby's care in some foster mother's house. All that time, I held onto the hope that the girl would be ours, that Mary would change her mind, claim the girl, bring her home. She is, of course, still ours, though I became sure that November morning that she had been, finally, legally, carried away.

It seemed fitting that she would go during this opening and closing time of the ancients. That morning in 1967, imagined the man and woman who were becoming her parents traveling through the fog, muffling every sound, even the earth insisting that everything take place behind the veil, must transpire in secret.

Every April and November, and every time the fog rolls in, and many of the days between, I think of her, wish to see her again, to feel, for the first time, the skin of her fingers wrapped around mine, the feel and sense of her no longer hidden. What has happened to her since I saw her no longer hidden. I wish to offer her what I can of our part of her story, of her people, which have been withheld from her.

Those first days and weeks and months of life, which should have been lovely, the beginning of her part of the story, may never be recovered. The church does not give up its workings lightly. I cannot make up for that loss, no matter how much I wish it. Still, I wish that she finds her way, when she is ready, back through the veil, to learn who she is and where she is from. To learn that she has always been loved.

Annalynn Seeks the Sky

Within Annalynn's whitewashed cottage, all is silent. In one of two small bedrooms, Annalynn blinks open her eyes, greets what counts for dark in the wee hours of a summer night near the top of the world. She holds her breath; she holds herself perfectly still. Her niece sleeps in the single bed in the room next to hers, as she has done in the two months since she arrived, unannounced and certainly not at Annalynn's request.

Not wanting to risk the noise that tossing off her covers would make, Annalynn slides out of from under them, fully clothed. Her boots wait at the foot of the bed. She lifts them, and then tiptoes, in stocking feet, toward the front door. Heart racing, she turns the knob slowly, pausing halfway round to listen again, before completing the turn. The click of the latch letting go screeches into the still air.

Outside, Annalynn closes the door quickly, hurries across the skinny road, a single lane that dead-ends at a view of the sea on the west coast of this island on which she has lived all of her eight decades. Behind the gorse that lines the field opposite her home, Annalynn looks to the sky, finds the moon, confirms its shape, waxing gibbous. She nods, heart slowing just a little with the reassurance that the phase of the moon she anticipated is the one that's there in the sky, waiting for her. She dares a small smile, then bends, slowly, slips on her boots; her knotted fingers require extra time to make the laces secure. When the task is complete, she turns inland, keeping to the edge of the road.

Not more than a mile along, she meets a lone sheep. She stops. The sheep advances. Annalynn squats beside her, a draft ewe, too old for rough grazing. Mutton soon. Annalynn laughs. *The pair of us.* The ewe's heft blocks the wind; she allows Annalynn close enough to look into her yellowed iris, the dark oval of pupil a gap in the rock through which the right person can slide. Annalynn rests there for a few minutes, gathering herself and making sure no one has followed before rising to her full height again and moving on.

She gains good ground. Her heart regains the pace it had when she opened the door. Now, though, it is her long, brisk stride that causes it. She quickens the pace, determined to gather as much space and time as she can. She imagines her niece waking, thumping into the kitchen, disheveled with sleep, brow furrowed at the water taking too long to boil on the old hob. How long until this happens? How long after that will it take her to notice Annalynn gone, gather her comrades, come for her? If they catch Annalynn this time, she will never be able to make this journey again.

Beyond the sign that alerts the tourists of the trail that leads to the Fairy Pools, Annalynn steps off the road, onto the moor. In the past, her error has been following the marked path. This time, she will follow the sheep track as far as she can. The sheep use the marked path primarily to leave prizes for the tourists, their muck clinging to the boots of the careless. Sheep have their own ways of navigating. Most people think sheep are utterly thick; she used to think so herself, before Niall went, before she had to make her way without him beside her.

Annalynn descends into the glen in the direction of the river, on the opposite side from the trail. There will have to be a crossing if she is to get where she wants. She marches for an hour, she guesses, judging by the lowering of the moon. She scales a lone outcropping of gneiss, black against the pre-dawn grey of the glen, barely enough to give her a vantage point. Crouched on top, she can see right the way back to the sign, its outline just visible. Hummocks of grass and sheep are her only companions. She continues the descent.

At the lowest point, hidden by rising rock and rolling hills on all sides, she relaxes, folding herself all to way down to the ground. On her back, ignoring the possibility of slugs and worms and the odd wee spider, she stares at the lowering moon.

What day is it?

This is what they always ask her. As far as she is concerned, only two days matter: *Diluain*, the name Niall gave days like these, using the original language, Gaelic. Monday, its translation. And didn't she and Niall have a Monday whenever they liked? What should she care whether it matches the tight squares on the calendar her niece has hung on the fridge? "To help you," she said. As though matching these things up sets the world to rights.

When the first slant of sun tilts up over the horizon, Annalynn is taken by a notion. She sits up. Dare she? If this is, indeed, her last chance to make a whole *Diluain,* she wants it all. She seeks the sky, most importantly, but why not gather all she can from the ground along the way? She reaches, and, as Niall used to, pulls off her boots and socks. A light wind grazes her skin as she peels off her skirt and knickers, blouse and slip. Her wrinkly wee titties no longer need a bra. She imagines the wind as Niall's soft kiss. Annalynn tiptoes to the edge of the granite-walled pool. She slides in; the clear water rises around her, ripples out. Her skin wavers beneath—hard to tell what is the pale aged flesh, still unfamiliar, and what's caused by the water, clear as it was when she was a girl. She submerges.

Soon, the tourists will amble up the path. She prefers to think of them instead of the others. Tourists won't stop her from getting what she needs. They will be too busy bleating about the black beauty ahead, the ancient rise of molten earth turned inside out. Few do the hard work required to get close enough to lay their hands on the gorgeous igneous protrusion, though. Such things are as rare as she would like *Dihaione*, the fast day, to be. She thinks a moment; Friday, isn't that what they call it now? The translation makes no sense to her—no one fasts anymore; they are afraid of hunger.

Annalynn draws herself up, pulls herself back to solid ground, gathers her boots and clothes. The air begins to dry her as she steps away from the path. She resists the impulse to turn and see if they are coming. Perhaps the sight of her bare bum would shock them to a standstill. Perhaps they would shout to her, the distance and the sky making their voices across the moor meaningless vibrations. They would say she is senile. A sure demonstration that she is walking in the wilds, in broad daylight no less, in her bare scud.

But who, she would like to ask them, who, in her right mind, would put clothes back on straight after climbing, soaking, out of a fairy pool?

"Who?" She calls to a huddle of sheep ahead of her, on the first rise up Bruach na Frithe.

Today, she must climb beyond the sheep. She looks up, to the place where the almost full moon will rise this evening. *Perfect.* She reaches up her hand, pink nail stretching high, white crescent aligning with the not-yet-set moon. She must reach the sky. She must complete a *Diluain.* She has tried time and again; someone always comes and pulls her back, making her life a constant *Dihaoine*—Friday, full of deprivation. Surely this time, she has gained enough ground ahead of them. She leans into the wind; she presses on.

Seventy years ago, a Monday, Niall first came to her parents' croft in the middle of a midsummer afternoon. He asked her to go a walk. All the islanders still spoke Gaelic, reserving their scant English for tourists, who had recently taken to bringing cars to the island then. Niall took her down to watch them come across on the ferry at Kylerhea.

"Do you fancy one?" she asked.

"I fancy you," he said.

She giggled.

They sat, side by side, long after the last car rumbled off up the curving road and the last pedestrian disappeared around the bend of the hills. They breathed in the breeze, the sound of the gulls overhead and each other. The sun had begun to lower before they rose for home.

Niall held her hand while she lifted her skirts above the damp hummocks of grass on the moor, there being neither signs nor clearly marked ways then. Despite the darkening sky, he steered her, not directly home, but upwards. As the soil dwindled and rock took over, she let her skirts go. She would have been steady enough on the climb all on her own; she suspected Niall knew it. His grip never loosened, though, nor did she pull her hand from his.

At the top, a clear night offered them the universe. They pointed, star to star, hands starting apart and then coming together.

"You are my north star," he said.

"You must be my moon," she said.

He came to her cottage again, exactly a week later, took her a different climb. At the top, clouds began to settle. Niall named them as they came: cumulus, nimbostratus, lowering and wrapping around them.

"Under here," he said, "Only I can find you."

Annalynn climbs, her skinny, aged limbs like birch with its peeling bark, stiff and determined. By now, even the less eager of the tourists will have risen in B&Bs and self-catering cottages all over her wee island. Soon, the land will bear the crash of them bumbling about, not noting what's underfoot or overhead. They will look from the guidebook to what's in front of them. Their eyes will land on what they've been told to see. They'll take photos, trudge on, checking the book or map or even the phone. Maybe they will glance at each other. The exception to this may be the very young and in love or lust, who still know how to see with hands and lips.

Annalynn knows the heat of hand in hand or rib to rib. She rubs her own permanently chilled hands together. She looks at the thin sun overhead. The tourists are easy enough to avoid, high as she is now. The others, who either know this island nearly as well as she, or know someone who does—they are her worry. She hesitates, thinking of her niece and the doctor, tourists in her life. They see her as a relic, think they have rights to climb all over her life, think they are protecting her, preserving her. For what? They think their ways are better; they think they know best; they think old women are no longer fit for seeking sky.

Not so very long after they began to walk out together, Niall went away onto the mainland. He'd finished the little island school. The brightest boy, they said, should do something better, should attend the university in Glasgow. People had been leaving a long time then. Sailing across the minch, south and away, escaping harsh winters and midge-filled summers and a hunger that never seemed to relent.

Until Niall went, Annalynn hadn't minded the hunger in herself. Just watching him go, though, she felt its claw, low in her belly. As the months passed, she began to think, like the others, that the way to be satisfied would be to go herself. Before she'd the chance to conjure a plan, Niall arrived, breathless, at her door, holding a fistful of primrose and violet.

They wanted to teach him about rock, make him a geologist. He wanted his hands on the rock.

"Not a fragment the size of your fist," he said. The other boys turned the specimens as though they were delicate butterflies. Niall wanted his hands, his feet, his whole body, connected to it.

"I want the living smell of it, for God's sake," he said. He leaned into her. "And I want you."

He tugged her out the front door, her apron still on. He named the rocks for her as they walked.

"They made us recite them from memory," he said. "As though naming makes things real."

Higher now, Annalynn rounds the corner that offers her the first glimpse of the gap in the rock that she must climb, hand over hand, to the place where she can lie still and meet the sky before they come with their grabbing hands and harsh language. She feels their words behind her, chasing.

"Don't be silly, Auntie Anna. Climbing. Alone. What are you thinking?" Her niece, going on and on in the car on the way to the doctor's the last time.

"What day is it Mrs. Gordon? What year? What date?" Doctor what's-her-name leaning in, skin smooth and smelling like sugar.

As though it matters.

"What size is the moon?" Annalynn replied. "What time did it rise? Waxing or waning?"

When they come this time, she will give answers. She will use their language to be sure they understand.

Friday, she will say. (Definitely not Monday if they are in it)

Third moonrise since Beltane, she will say. *Saturn rising*. In case they need more.

Almost full, she will say. *Waxing*.

A January night, not long after they married, Niall came to her by the fire, took her hand, in the time before they knew that there would be no children. She rose to meet him, trusting whatever it was—maybe another try for the bairns. They tried often; they tried more once the truth settled, the need to connect seeming more urgent, as though they had to count the times like beads on the rosary. This is what she expected when Niall rose that January night. He stood still, though, both his hands in hers. He held her eyes too.

"Fancy another Monday?" he asked.

It was Sunday. She nodded anyway, not quite sure what he meant, imagining Mondays stretching out behind her like a trawler's wake.

Monday: Mam hanging the wash on the line.

Monday: Aileen at the back door, caught having a fag.

Monday: Da thumping in, mucky boots. But that was every other day as well.

Her twin sisters, weren't they Monday's children?

She rumpled her brow.

"Diluain," Niall whispered.

Monday: Niall at the door, that first time: "Can Annalynn come a walk?"

Of course. *Diluain.* Day of the moon.

Her face softened. Niall pulled her in, not so much as to be visible, just enough to let her know he had seen and understood, a silent answer in the way that he answered her most often: with fingers and eyes, and, when he did answer with lips, not in the way that needed words.

Outside they found the sky had darkened early, it having been a low hanging sort of a day in which neither night nor sky had fully lifted. They tottered along the sheeptrack, torches stuffed in their pockets—this in the time when only miners wore headlamps—so their hands would be free for each other. At the top of a peak Niall hadn't shown her before, they turned off their lights, curled under blankets, against each other; they nuzzled and dozed. Annalynn woke, lay still under the moon, the night and the sky and Niall's arm wrapped around her.

He took her farther afield, too. Once, they went all the way to America to see the twins, who had sailed over after the war, written of a third-story flat, two Scottish families living underneath them. They had had enough money leftover to buy a real coconut for seventeen cents, whatever that meant. They cracked it open, and each drank the milk of it sitting on the floor of the flat, that high up it was nearly in the sky, they wrote. She and Niall read the letter together. They turned toward each other at the line about the sky. They smirked and read on.

At the end, she put the letter neatly back into its envelope. Niall smoothed her hair, stood, reached high for a rarely-used jar, dug in his pocket, put in a whole sovereign, nodded.

It took them eleven years to have enough to go across. By then, each twin had a house, a husband and a daughter of her own, near the pebbled shores of Maine. It was hard, they said, living in a place you couldn't walk from coast to coast. The rocks and the seaweed seemed a bridge to where they'd started. The daughters danced and sang for their strange aunt and uncle come across the waters. "Where are your children?" one girl asked, before one mother shushed her.

Feet now on the rock beyond the grass, Annalynn wonders was it worth it, that trip? The daughter who was shushed is here on the island now; it is she who has brought Annalynn back to Friday after Friday.

"And where are your children?" Annalynn wants to ask. Children might at least distract her. The niece wants to take Annalynn with her to Maine. She'd been told, by whom Annalynn hasn't sussed, about Annalynn's walks, day and night. She came to see for herself, a semester sabbatical, she said.

Annalynn knows nothing of semesters or sabbaticals. She knows the turn of the days and the nights, the flow of the moon, the rinse of colored lights in the skies that mark the high points of seasons. She learned these from Niall, who pointed them out to her in the sky. She keeps them now, without Niall.

Since that last walk with Niall, since his fall not even halfway up Bruach na Frithe, she has kept them alone. There he was, ahead of her, hand warm around hers. And then he was on the ground, eyes too wide and wild, one, hand grasping his chest, the other reaching for hers. She began to pull away, to search for help; she looked wildly back across the moor, eyes like a sheep's, unblinking, a desperate bleating inside her.

"Stay..." he gasped.

She bent then, lowered her face to his, felt his hand slacken as their lips met. The doctor said his heart had given all it could. Only Annalynn knows this to be false: she has held Niall and his heart in hers as she has marked each of the fifty-two constellations, nearly one full turn of the earth, all without his body beside her.

Annalynn knows she has forgotten much. No matter how hard she looks and whispers to herself, she cannot keep the things she learns now. She doesn't understand why anyone is surprised by this. How would she be able to keep anything without Niall nuzzling it into her, to seal it with his arms and eyes and lips, after all these years, nearing seventy of them now?

She has learned enough at any rate. She never needed a whole grand continent; she'd the details of her own wee island and Niall, and of the sky if she needed something bigger.

Annalynn recites the few names she can recall as she places her hands on the rock. *Gabbros*, she thinks, *igneous*. Then, *Diluain*. Just the name of it doesn't make it real. *The name makes it a possibility.* Her boots on the soil, hands on solid stone, the dark scent rising in her nostrils, those make the day real. Those make her real.

She imagines them now, her niece and an orderly and who knows who else, behind her, clucking to each other the words they have said to her. *You could get hurt.* As though she has lived these eight decades without a scratch. As though a fall is the worst hurt a life can offer. *You could get lost.* As though she has suddenly become a tourist. As though she doesn't know how to read the signs. *You're not young anymore.*

"Old," she said it for them, last time. "Near enough ancient. Annalynn the Ancient." She chuckled. Her niece blushed.

Soon, the niece will have her way and take her. There will be the scent of seaweed, the sharp-edged rocks, the other side of the same moon. There will be no new Mondays—how could there be, so far from the path along which the memory of Niall guides her?

Annalynn holds Niall within her as she pulls herself, hand over hand, pale skin ridged as though it has been worn by the same ancient lava flow as the ridge she climbs. She sees Niall's hand ahead of her, as it was that first time, pulling her. She feels Niall watching her haul her body, now lined like the black rock. She leaves everything else behind, carrying only the idea that he sees her now, she like a pale porphyritic outcropping, a crystal larger than those in the rock, the perfect texture.

After the clouds landed on them that second time, Niall smiled at her. The sky had come to them, become a veil hiding them from view. Niall bent, asked with his eyes, kissed her long and deep and unashamed. She blinked, red-faced and unsure, when he pulled away. He cupped her chin in his hands. “Ah love. It’s okay. We can do whatever we like when we’re part of the sky.”

Between Sea and Sky

It's seventy years ago now, and still she remembers what it was to feel her father's rhythm at the start of a day, to eat with him and walk with him and feel the flow of his voice, deep and rough, rolling over her, to watch him push away from the shore and to think nothing of it. The eldest of five, and, like her father, not in need of much rest, Agatha often found herself awake with him while her mother and her sisters slept. She and Da stepped into the dark of many mornings, the scent of seaweed pushing in on the wind and the smell of the dark muck and dung rising to fill their noses and lungs, and to wake them fully as they lifted, with winter-worn hands, rough turves of peat, dried and stacked neatly outside. Inside again, they rebuilt the fire Da smothered before bed every night while her sisters tucked into each other, filling the space Agatha had left. Across the cottage, alone in the bed she shared with Da, Agatha's mother curled into herself.

In those days, in their cottage and most of the others on Skye, you saw a man's head first. The thatched roofs hung low, forcing the doors to be built even lower, so anyone of much height, meaning any man and a good many women were forced to hunch and, before his body hurried in after him, present his face. This is what Agatha's father did after his day of work, and men like Angus Donald, who flipped off his grey cap and let his black hair unfurl into their cottage before he pulled in his body and took his seat by the fire. As the flames flickered, never quite as large or as warm as they might have liked, the men told tales about those they claimed had built cottages like theirs on the west of Skye, the little people, fairies, in the days when it had been safe for them to be seen on the land, before they'd been forced to live within the hills. It seemed obvious to Agatha, though, that the low-slung shelters just made sense—the thatch not too high to patch and the ceilings low enough to hold down around them the heat from the fire and from their own selves and the breath of whoever was the tale teller of the night.

Before it was theirs, the cottage belonged to Agatha's mother's family. Her grandparents claimed it when they brought their family to an easier life, sailing away from where generations of them had lived, twelve miles further out to sea on The Shiant Isles. They brought with them the clothes on their backs and their resilience and their tales, gathered from myths of the great Celtic warriors, men like Ossian and Cuchulain and women like Sgiathaich—The Warrior Queen, and from their own families.

Of all the tales, the one Agatha's mother most often asked her father to tell was not any of the Celtic warriors or queens, but of themselves, concerning their first encounter on Skye, after both families had moved. When Da told it, he referred to himself by his whole name, as though he was telling it about another person entirely.

"Calum Stuibhart could not recall a day without Morag McLeod," he'd begin. "Until, that is, the moment his father made him and the rest of the Stuibharts huddle into their boat and roll over the waters to Skye."

Although in later tellings, Da spoke in English, he preferred the rhythm of the Gaelic as he told of the waters that looked like the great Cuillin mountains near which they would settle, dark grey and jagged and under caps of freezing white.

"A strapping lad of thirteen," he went on, "with nearly black hair and flinty eyes but tall already and broad, young Calum pined for the lovely Morag."

Months, it took them, first on the waters and then searching for a cottage and repairing the thatch and cutting and drying and stacking the peat and all the other loads of things he'd to do to help his father make the new life they wanted on Skye. Through all of it, Calum imagined Morag's thick, auburn hair, her waist, already taking the shape of a young woman, her freckled hands. Though he'd known her from their youngest years, he realized in those months of cutting and stacking and thatching that he missed her in a different way than he missed the others he'd either left behind on The Shiants or been separated from on Skye. He began, too, to think of all the new lads on Skye whom she might be meeting.

"Young Calum worked harder," he said, "looking for the day his own father would be satisfied that they'd made a good start and allow Calum to roam free for a bit." He tried not to think about the fact that there were likely thousands of boys his age on Skye, rather than the few in the ten-or-so families with whom he'd shared The Shiants. And he tried to work away his fear that one such boy could have distracted Morag, perhaps even making her forget Calum altogether.

"Three months, Calum had, to think about Morag and whether she'd forgotten him and what he might do to make sure she remembered him over whatever others might come to meet her. By the time his father turned to him, a turve of peat in his hand and said, 'Well done, lad. Away you go and have some fun,' Calum knew precisely what he'd do.

"He ran up over the hill and down to the shore, pinched a rowing boat not nearly sturdy enough for Skye's southwestern waters, whose moods change faster than a toddler. Calum was equal parts luck and determination, though, and made the most of both to reel in three salmon so big they looked as though they'd been about those waters long enough to think themselves safe from man and bird. With these fish in hand, Calum Stuibhart replaced what could then be safely called a borrowed vessel and marched himself from the rocks, across the field to Morag's cottage. Upon encountering the low-slung door, Calum first thrust through the fish and then his face, ducking as though he was already a man."

Da told how he found Morag and her brother and sister hunched by the fire. Her father mended a net at the table and her mother stood mixing the flour and butter to make a dough.

"Is mise Calum Stuibhart. Ciamar a tha sibh." I'm Calum Stuart. How are you?

"Tha mi gu math." Morag giggled, saying she was well.

"De an t'aimn a tha oirbh?" he asked, as though he hadn't known her name from its very beginning.

"Is mise Morag." She threw her hair back over her shoulder and stood.

I am happy to know you, he said, still using the formal Gaelic.

Agatha's grandfather might have thought him soft in the head and sent him packing had he not had those fish, which were then duly cleaned and gutted and smoked. Calum was, of course, not only invited to stay and partake of them, but celebrated as the provider of fresh flesh in the middle of a harsh winter.

They would be married before he brought more fish like that to Agatha's mother, but when he did, he did as he had that first time, presenting the fish and ducking his head and removing his cap as though he was a stranger come courting and introducing himself afresh in hopes of winning the lassie's heart. "Is mise Calum Stuibhart," and always ending the exchange as he had that first time: I am happy to know you.

This began a tradition that continued whenever Agatha's father came through the door with an especially good catch.

There is no need, these long decades later, for Agatha to duck her head when she passes through what used to be the doorway of the cottage. The roof is gone; one wall has crumbled almost to the ground. Agatha paces off the interior edges of the cottage, her hand in the air next to the wall or the gaps in it, formed in her absence, as though to trace it. She sits in the space that held the bed on which she and her sisters slept. (If she lay down here, pulled her jacket around her tightly, pressed her head to the floor, who would come looking?) She recalls lying there, body warm in the blankets, face chilled, hearing her father whisper to Angus Donald, who'd stayed too late the night before to make his way back to the village.

"Angus, how's about a bit of fresh?"

She needn't open her eyes to know that they sat, already, side by side by the fire.

"Is it not too cold?"

"Ah come on, just the pair of us, gaining on the waters and the wind and bringing a wee surprise, eh? A lovely belly warmer?"

Her mouth tingled, the memory of a bit of freshness rekindled just at the time when she feared she might have lost altogether the feel of tender flesh against her tongue. They were, by then, more than a month past the solstice and the night had begun to part earlier and allow the day in longer. Still, though, it was a long way to spring.

The full moon and the nearly clear skies drew the pair of men to the waters. Agatha wanted to be any part of it that she could. She slid out and over to the fire and felt her da's hand, calluses catching in her hair. "You'll be wanting to help, then, doithín," he said. "You'll keep our secret—let her try to suss for herself where we've gone." He nodded over to her mother. "If I'm lucky, I'll have a great big catch before she's sorted it out."

Agatha pulled on her sheepskin mittens, struggling against a sudden gust of wind to wrap extra woolens around her. She tramped, guided as much by memory as by their lanterns or the moon, down to the shore with them.

Agatha rises now, following her own old steps, taking care to look before each footfall. Funny, she thinks, how her memory can guide her to the precise spot on the shore, but each movement of the foot must now be watched to be sure her body properly connects with land, propels her forward instead of resulting in a fall.

She sits just to the edge of the place where she gave her father and Angus a last push with all her might and watched them row away into a perfect light breeze. It wasn't the season, but it wouldn't be the first time her father had come in with a fistful of salmon when others came back with nothing but a salty burn on their faces and empty nets in their hands.

Just after midday, Agatha finished spinning the last of the yarn that had been cleaned and carded after the last shearing. Her mother stood at the table, making bannock but flinging flour when she should have been letting it settle, thinking Da had gone away into Carbost with Angus. The two sisters closest in age to Agatha had already run off, over the hill somewhere. The baby stood on a stool, side by side with her mother, imitating her every flail of the arm. Agatha made her escape then, down to the rocks in search of some good skipping stones and maybe a glimpse of Da and Angus, making their way back in the distance. She found a good perch and a few lovely flat stones and Dairmid MacKimmon as well.

Dairmid and she had been born on the same day, he in the cottage by the shore and she in hers. His mother took ill and so her mother nursed them both for months. When the time came for him to go and sleep in his own house, the pair of them were said to have keened louder than a caoineag, a witch who visits in dreams and visions, crying out a portent of death. Dairmid and Agatha kept their keening going and refused food until they were brought back to each other. She had no memory of a day without Dairmid, and, that day, they threw stone after stone, not having the need of saying anything. They could have gone on like that for hours, only something caught her eye, a dark patch on the sea. She watched it spread, whitecaps rise, and she pointed. Dairmid lifted his cap and they both sat, staring at the black clouds reaching long wisps like witches' fingers down to the waters, seeming to call the sea skyward. Something shifted in her gullet, low, and she thought she should maybe spoil the surprise, tell her mother that her father wasn't gone to the village, back to Angus' house after all. She stood.

She told Dairmid she had spinning yet to finish and turned back toward the cottage, still small enough to make it through the door upright.

As though she didn't believe it, Agatha's mother set out in the direction of the shore. Agatha went behind and saw her mother find the boat missing, smile and then look out to the sea, the squall already gone, "Is mise Calum Stuibhart."

Agatha's mother took to an extra sweeping out of the cottage and another milking of the cow, to take up the time until her father came. When the night began to creep in, she went down the shore with her light and waited, as she had so often, to guide her husband in.

After the dark settled in fully, Agatha went to the rocks. Her mother, silent and still, held the lantern high and her face straight out toward the sea. She did not shift even her eyes to acknowledge her daughter there. The wind lifted their hair, swept in under their shawls, rising as it often did with the moon at that time of year, gathering chill from the waters beside her, blowing steadily, which made her somehow comfortable in it.

As Agatha made her way over the rocks toward Dairmid's cottage, though she felt hurried, her movements appeared fluid and unpanicked.

Dairmid's father opened the cottage door. "Young Agatha." He smiled.

Dairmid turned from banking the fire, rose, knowing she should have been scraping the scales off some big, bulgy-eyed fish by then. "Is he not back?"

In the time it took her to shake her head and turn outward again, Dairmid and his father had on their heavy sweaters and boots and caps. In the time it took her to get back to the cottage and send word to Angus' family in Carbost, Dairmid and his father had their own lanterns lit and were pushing away from the shore. Her stomach clenched at the sight of them, even though she knew they'd hug the crannies of the coastline and leave the further out places to a bigger vessel and more men from the village, if necessary. The smell of seaweed cut into her, no longer seeming fresh and full of possibility, but overwhelmingly pungent and salty, like aged winter meats; it wrapped around her, a clinging slimy scent that would not release.

The next morning and early afternoon, she scuttled back and forth between her mother and the cluster of larger rocks at the edge of the bay, resisting the impulse to jump into the waters herself and swim until she found them. When she could no longer stand neither being able to do nor see, she climbed the hill on the south edge of the bay, scrambling along the path the sheep made, slipping more than once, her hands landing in watery grass and dark muck or sheep dung. She didn't care so long as she was moving to a better vantage point.

From the top she could see west and south easily and a little north up the minch between Skye and Lewis. She watched the trawler from the village pass inward, men scurrying about on board. Below her, Dairmid's mother came out and wrapped a blanket around her mother. Through the lot of it, Agatha's mother stood, lantern in hand, not moving even as the tide came in around the rocks, bringing closer and closer the idea that Da was gone.

Agatha watched Dairmid climb toward her, his head angled toward his feet as though it was his first time on the land. When he reached the top, he stood close, his jacketed shoulder catching her dark shawl. He handed her a pebble, smooth and flat, opened his palm to show he had one as well. Together, they cast them out, watched them fall to the wide waters, too far below to hear when they sank. Dairmid plunged his hands into his pockets, lifted his shoulders earward. "My ma says I've to tell you to tend your sisters."

She did as she was told, though when she got there, she found there was no need; someone, or they themselves, had tucked them into the big bed and smothered the fire. She lifted the peat and built it back, as though it was morning again, as though she'd hear his whisper, as though they could just start that day fresh. She sat the night there, where she'd last felt her father's hand and voice on her. She dozed a little, and wakened to the faint whisper of the wind rising with the sun.

She looked over the beds, counted four on the big one and none on the other. She forgot about starting the porridge and went, instead, to the rocks. Her mother stood there still, keening by then for the one soul who knew her beyond the marrow, straight through to the rock and the roaring air that made her who she was. Agatha's mother stood through the day's search and until darkness fell again, still weeping, whispering, "Is mise Calum," again and again until she fell into the arms of a man from the village whose name Agatha did not know, come to offer condolences. He carried her up the hill and tucked her in beside the other girls.

In the morning, while her mother still slept, Agatha lined the sisters up in front of the fire and told them their father had been claimed by the sea, that he wasn't bringing fish or himself across their threshold again.

"D'you mean he's been caught?" This from Mairi, then five.

"Caught?"

"Aye. Instead of him catching the fishes, they've caught him."

"You might say. Not the fishes though, but the waters themselves have taken him."

Mairi nodded as though she understood and then her face turned to tears. She gasped. "Will they scrape him and split open his tummy and cook him?"

"Ah no doithín." Agatha pulled Mairi into her, sitting on the floor in front of the fire. "It's not like that at all. He's only gone into the waters, become part of the lovely waters now, instead of being part of us."

She fell silent then. Young Morag joined her on Agatha's knee and Anna tucked in on the other side. Aileen, only two years younger than Agatha, climbed back into bed with their mother.

Mairi brightened a bit and said, "Maybe our da will become a selkie and come back to us." Da had told many a selkie story there by the fire; conjured tales of the magical creatures who came onto land and captured the hearts of men or women and lured them out to sea.

Dairmid's mother saved Agatha having to spoil Mairi's fantasy of not only having her father back but of him also being magical when he came. She came along with Dairmid behind, carrying food for them as though they'd none already put away for winter. Agatha's mother slept through them and several others, only sitting up at dusk and sliding out from under the blankets and taking her lantern down to wait by the rocks until the dark settled completely. When she came back in, she stood and stared at the five girls by the fire as though she wasn't sure how they'd arrived there.

"You'll want your tea," she said, and set the lantern on the table, all that electric energy she'd had before suddenly gone, depleted by trying to will her husband back from the sea.

Three days later, while Agatha's mother waited with her lantern, the sea delivered to an inlet just southwest, one splintered oar, not near any known hideaway for fish of any sort. The waters would not return the bodies of Agatha's father or of Angus or any other piece of their boat. Her mother moved through those days as though she was no more in her body than Da must have been by then, coming back to herself as the night began to settle and marching to the rocks to keen and light the way for a man who could no longer see.

It fell to Agatha, the eldest, ten years ahead of the youngest, to become something between mother and father whilst her own mother stood still, her tears washing among the tide flowing in around the rocks. It fell to Agatha to slide from bed before light and wrest from the stack the peat that had been cut and dried and stacked by her father's hands during the summer. She lifted that peat that had last been touched by him, imagining that touching the peat with her hand was as good as touching his own hand. She stepped into his footprints, back to the cottage, over to the fire, handling the tools that had been his to make the fire roar, ready for her mother to awaken and lift the pot of oats that had been soaking overnight. Except her mother slept, so after Agatha put her hands and feet where her father had put his, she did the same for her mother, making the porridge hot in the morning and helping move them through the days until it was time to tuck in her sisters at night and then to smother the fire and the day.

These things and more fell to her and so, by the third day she decided that it also fell to her to dig from her mother's treasure box under her bed, the address of her Aunt Wina and Uncle Donagh and to write to them, in Glasgow, to say that her father was dead. Would she have written had she known they would come to Skye and take them all away back to Glasgow, and that it would take her exactly seventy years to get back?

Agatha presses to standing, there on the rocks. Her knees crackle. Gulls circle overhead. One swoops low, calling as though berating her for failing to bring something from which a crumb or two might fall. She steps to the edge.

February waters, the same grey green, lap at her feet, cold enough to feel through wellington boots and thick socks she spun and knit decades ago, darned again and again to keep them functional. She uncoils the rope, heaves it into the little boat, cranes her neck slightly to make sure both oars are there.

Her fingers gain leverage against an edge of wood on the bow. *Clinker built.* The details return as she feels the smooth against her hands. She lifts. She watches her feet disappear as she steps across the seaweed and in, placing the little skiff—*sgoth niseach*—in the perfect amount of water to allow it to remain stable enough for her to enter, yet become buoyant with one mighty shove of oar against pebbled sea floor. She pushes back a wisp of long, white hair and with it the tickle of a thought that, had she waited another year, she might not have had the strength to lift the bow far enough or plant the oar firmly enough to roll out, as she does now, against the tide.

She takes her time. She has plenty of it after all. She can wander between sea and sky for as long necessary, until she finds the place where the waters will give her what she needs.

Jessie Finds Herself

Sunlight, strained through stained glass, casts red and green and orange on the heads of rows of parishioners. Jessie fixes on a watery blue cast not by the Glory-Be-To-God windows, but by the hairdressers of this Scottish seaside village. Sitting with her spine so straight as to make the wooden pews seem slouched, Jessie usually attends the sermon fully, focusing on each word arching out of Reverend Williams' mouth, landing without a splash.

Today, the minister talks of families. As he goes on about growing the congregation with youth, increasing the numbers of children in the crèche and grandchildren who visit, the words seem to dribble down his chin rather than diving elegantly outward. Jessie's younger son died years ago, hardly having fully committed himself to being thirty-something. His wife took their daughter somewhere Jessie was unable to follow.

Jessie wiggles her toe secretly in her polished black shoe, thinking of her other son, who has taken a far-off promotion and her grandchildren with it. She thinks of them across the Atlantic; thinks maybe she'll stroll down to the shore after the service and look at the ocean's calm blue on this sunny day. It's then, as she tries to pull her attention back inside, back to the spray of the sermon, that she realizes she's already amid a sea of blue. Curled blue heads dot nearly every row of pew, front to (she dares a half turn of her head) back.

As she has the thought, the rolling waves of blue-haired ladies rise to sing on the minister's command. Jessie stands too, of course, briefly thinking how the minister's walk down the aisle at the end of the service must look a wee bit like the parting of the waters as each blue wave turns its face toward him. Jessie banishes the blasphemy, absently patting her head and so realizing that she, too, is a wave.

Perhaps because of the sermon, she thinks first of the children. She has told those grandchildren repeatedly, "Be an individual." She's known the value of this since childhood; learning it by watching her mother bring her and her four sisters from World War I to adulthood without heading to the parish line, ever. They held their heads above the tide of poverty by thinking for themselves. That's what she's tried to teach her grandchildren.

Jessie sings along with the hymn, resists the urge to turn her head with the rest of the waves when the minister passes. She slides out of the pew behind the others, a tide changing direction.

Outside, she glances up at the sky, forgets the stroll. She wants to check the calendar, to confirm that she's a hair appointment on Tuesday. She thinks of the other ladies under the dryers, blue setting into their silver hair. She pictures herself, separate, stepping out after, no longer one of the rolling blue waves but a newly released white crest.

Acknowledgements

I'm both grateful and delighted that my books have found a home at Vine Leaves Press; thank you, Melanie Faith, Jessica Bell, and Amie McCracken for your tremendous time, hearts, and talents.

I am also grateful to the publications where many of these stories first found a home: "Substrata" in *New Writing Scotland 31, Black Middens*; "Clear Blue Line" and "Within" in the *Emrys Journal*, Volumes 21 and 26; "Understory" in *Pine Mountain Sand & Gravel, Volume 17, Tricksters, Truthtellers and Lost Souls,* and in *Quarried,* an anthology of the best of three decades of *Pine Mountain Sand & Gravel*; "Payline" in *Words from an Island, Number 1, Island Life*; "When the Crust Breaks" in *Words from an Island Number 2, A Stillness of Mind*; "Celestial Navigation" in the *Masters Review*; "Between Sea and Sky" in *Northwords Now*, Issue 20, "Behind the Veil," excerpted from *When the Ocean Flies;* and "Between Sea and Sky," excerpted from *The Thorn Tree.*

Thank you, Maureen Nery, for being an early reader of this collection and for countless other hours of critiquing, encouragement, and general wisdom sharing.

Elaine Hadden, for reading, encouragement (really, cattle-prodding me through the rough spots), and, of course, for friendship.

And to dear friends who, during this publication cycle, in addition to their usual delight and support, held me up when my house was (literally) falling down, especially Chantal Haskell and Eric Anderson, Chip and Carol Radford, Nick and Casey Williams, Mimi Watson, Brooke Honeycutt, Jean Shew, Jonna Hamrick, Nilly Barr.

Always, I'm grateful for family, particularly Stewart Marshall, Corey Magruder, Dylan Magruder, Davis Hedges and Elizabeth Ross, Alan and Jackie Marshall, Rod and Ann Hawkins, Cailyn, Connor, and Laton.

Also by Heather G. Marshall

The Thorn Tree
When the Ocean Flies

Vine Leaves Press

Enjoyed this book?
Go to *vineleavespress.com* to find more.
Subscribe to our newsletter:

www.ingramcontent.com/pod-product-compliance
Lightning Source LLC
LaVergne TN
LVHW030921080826
845145LV00013B/2997

* 9 7 8 3 9 8 8 3 2 2 2 4 1 *